High
ALERT

BECCA SEYMOUR

RAINBOW TREE PUBLISHING

HIGH ALERT

BECCA SEYMOUR

RAINBOW TREE PUBLISHING

For information, contact the author: hello@beccaseymour.com

Editing: Hot Tree Editing

Cover Designer: BookSmith Design

Publisher: Rainbow Tree Publishing

E-book ISBN: 978-1-922359-89-6

Paperback ISBN: 978-1-922359-93-3

1

———

ROSS

THE GUYS WERE LATE. NERVES DANCED ALONG my spine, and I was sure the jocks I'd put on this morning had a hole in them, courtesy of my goat Benji. He was a regular hoodlum who had a taste for undies.

But the state of me wearing possibly holey boxers was indicative of the distracted state of my mind.

The sound of an engine dragged my gaze in its direction. My heart sped up, threatening to burst out of my chest *Alien*-style. My reaction was out of control. It was crazy—being so worked up about Dan coming home. Two years wasn't a long time in the scheme of things since I'd last seen him, which was when he'd last visited his parents. Not living in the same town as each other for thirteen years was doing a number on me.

But seeing Dan again this time was different.

Everything had changed.

Okay, so not so much "everything," since my crush remained the same. The difference was this time I could possibly do something about it.

Possibly.

Maybe.

In my sweetest and wildest of dreams.

The squeal of brakes had me exhaling. Any minute now, he'd be stepping out of my brother's Toyota. With just a few metres and steel between us, I had no idea how to react, not with the nervous excitement thrumming in my veins.

The doors opened, and movement caught my attention. Dan Madison followed after my brother, his eyes already on mine.

His hand tightened around the pack of beers he carried, and pink coloured his cheeks.

But that was likely my imagination making a much bigger deal about this reunion than it really was.

Funny, the things you noticed, though. He had new glasses. They were thicker rimmed than any style I'd seen him wear before. He rocked the whole hot geek vibe. Killed it, in fact.

Though there was nothing geeky about him in the traditional sense. Not when he worked with his hands for a living as a carpenter, and I doubted so much had changed that he wasn't digitally challenged beyond a game on the Xbox.

It took everything in me not to allow my gaze to eat him up.

Two years—however brief on that one-week visit home—of not working side by side with the man when I talked him into fitting me some new doors.

Two years of not listening to his addictive laugh that made me smile so big my face hurt.

And two years since once again, he'd left me disappointed when he'd waved goodbye and headed back to the city—and his boyfriend—where he'd set himself up with a new life away from the Sunshine Coast hinterland.

Never once had I told him about how I felt, the right time never seeming to arrive. If I'd known he was gay before he'd left town when he was twenty, perhaps I would have been more obvious with my crushing. At eighteen, I'd been very definitely out. But Dan's sexuality came as a surprise. Craig had dropped that bombshell when I was in my second year of uni.

And hadn't that been a kick in the gut, swiftly followed by elation. For the first time ever, I'd considered that just maybe I had a chance.

The chance never came, though.

There was no point when we lived a couple of hours apart. Long-distance wasn't something I thought I could handle, even when it was for my brother's best friend, the man who'd snagged a piece of my heart when my balls first dropped and my dick had thickened watching Gerard Butler in 300.

There was also the fact he'd *had* a boyfriend. *Had* been the exciting word of the day. Almost a year ago, they'd split.

The gravel under his feet grew louder, and his gaze remained fixed to mine. Barely a metre apart, and he stopped, shifting the six-pack to his side.

"Hey, Ross." Pretty light-brown orbs peered back at me, wide and just as mesmerising as I remembered. "Bloody hell, you're a sight for sore eyes."

I grinned, uncertain of the words that might fall out of my mouth.

I didn't need to worry. In Dan's next breath, he said, "Get your arse over here already and give me a hug."

I ignored my brother's snort as he snagged the beer from Dan and walked on past us.

A deep exhale escaped my lungs as I stepped forwards and pulled him into my arms. I wrapped myself around him, holding him tight. The feel of his large limbs, strong and firm, wrapped around my own frame made my heart sing.

"Good to see you too, mate. About time you made the move back to civilisation." My grin remained wide when I eased away, his snort making me chuckle.

"Civilisation, huh?"

"Yep. You better believe it. You know, a Subway opened in town, and Bunnings got an extension. Civilisation at its best."

Dan's laugh washed over me like a familiar hug, the sensation warming me, much like the log fire already built in my sitting room did.

"Come on." I gripped his arms, giving a happy squeeze. "Let's go and grab one of those beers."

He followed me inside, where we located my brother in the kitchen. Three beer bottles were already open, and Craig hovered next to the slow cooker, spoon in hand. "Oi, hands off the stew."

Craig whipped his head in my direction,

quirking his brow at me. "I'm using a spoon, not my fingers."

"I don't care if you use a gold ladle, just back off, else I'll serve you the dregs."

"Maybe we should do that anyway," Dan said as he picked up his beer. "Gives us first dibs and over-filled bowls."

"Bloody hell. And so it begins. You two together are a pain in my arse." My brother rolled his eyes at the pair of us. "Making it clear now, you two are not ganging up on me."

"What?" Mock innocence coloured my words. It was true though. Even though they were best mates, they'd always included me when we were kids and during every visit since then. Dan also had my back growing up, often picking my side even when I didn't deserve it, as I was a pain in my brother's arse.

I appreciated it, nonetheless.

"No idea what you're talking about, mate." Dan took a seat, his gaze roaming the kitchen. "We need to fix this room up." He cast a look at me.

I snorted. "Maybe... perhaps settle into your place and your new job first, and then I'll put you to work."

Dan bobbed his head, though the smirk indicated he'd be looking at fitting out the kitchen as soon as he wanted to. He could be a pushy bugger at times, but always with the best of intentions.

Over the next couple of hours, we ate and chatted about Dan settling back in, Craig's recent promotion at work and how things were going with his love life, and the diversity initiative I spearheaded at work. The whole time I appreciated how lucky I was to be so close to my brother, and while my feelings for Dan were far more than friendship, I classed him as a good friend. Even after all these years.

That was obvious as each minute passed by.

"Do you remember Mr Whittaker?" Dan asked when we'd fallen into talking about high school.

"You know, he only left Mitchell Oak two years before I started work there." This was my seventh year working at the same school that I'd attended as a teenager, but as school librarian rather than teacher.

"No shit?" Dan chuckled. "Bloody hell, he was ancient when we were at school. How'd he manage a few more years after that?"

"Right. He didn't retire till he was in his early seventies, I think. No idea how he lasted that long." I started clearing up our empty ice-cream bowls and stacked them in the dishwasher.

"And Mrs Bramble. You remember when she did that science experiment in assembly and it went wrong, blowing up?" Craig said, putting away the placemats. "Those dicks... what were their names from the year below us, who caused a stink, made it a nightmare for her?"

I lost my smile, immediately knowing who he was talking about. Every time I thought about my time at school, specifically after I'd come out, unpleasant memories slammed into me. It had taken many counselling sessions when I was at uni to help me let that time go.

The experience, though, had left its mark.

Neither Craig nor Dan knew the half of it.

Over ten years had passed since my year from hell—the year after my brother graduated school. The year that the group he was referring to refused to simply let me be.

I kept my mouth shut as they spoke, not needing to get involved with this blast of memories.

"Shit, what were their names?" Dan said like an annoying dog with a bone. "Jamie? But there was also that other kid who was a shit-stirrer."

Craig started spouting off names. "Nathan, Ricky?"

I expelled a frustrated breath, wanting them to put this conversation to bed. Grudgingly, I said, "Nick," the name I didn't think I'd ever forget.

"That's the one. God, he was a cockhead." Craig pulled another beer from the fridge and offered me one. I took it gratefully.

When I sat, I glanced over at Dan, whose focus was on me. The crease between his brows was prominent.

"What's wrong?" I asked.

His gaze searched mine. "Wasn't he the guy who started giving you shit before we left?"

I rolled my eyes and forced a laugh. "Bloody hell. You're asking me about something that happened, what, fifteen years ago?"

As soon as the words were out of my mouth, I realised my mistake.

Both of them knew I had the memory of an elephant. That fact was frustrating at times, like now when I feigned being oblivious.

They'd immediately wonder why I was pleading ignorance. They were worse than old Maeve at the local post office when getting information out of someone.

The worst thing was, me hiding any of this had never felt strange before, mainly because I'd sucked up my year in the eleventh grade. I'd had a decent final year in Year 12 though, which was something, once Nick and his gang had left.

That it bugged me now, in all honesty, pissed me off.

"So, plans tomorrow? You still up for a spot of fishing over at Lake Neverfill?"

That I changed the topic wouldn't be lost on either of them. But for whatever reason, Dan let it slide, saying, "Yeah. Early start, though. Setting our alarm for six?"

I could have kissed him for going with it. Though, I could have happily kissed him anyway just because he was hot as hell and one of the best men I knew.

"Six, really? It's Sunday. What happened to our lie-in?" Craig grumbled.

"Suck it up, sunshine. The early worm catches the fish."

I squinted at Dan.

"Yes, I know I butchered the phrase. I'm not the only one good with words." One of his brows shot high, and I grinned, more than happy to tease and let my high school memories go.

"Uh-huh, let's just stick with 'butchered,' shall we?"

"Okay, wise guy, we can do that. Let me grab my charger out of my bag and sort my alarm now before I have another drink and reconsider waking up early." I watched as he shoved his socked feet in his boots at the side of the back door. "Which room am I in?"

"The one next to mine. Craig's got the green room."

Craig groaned. "You seriously need to do something about the colour of that room, Ross. It makes me feel like I'm gonna throw up whenever I stay in it."

I smirked. "You're the one who stays in there the most. Pick a colour, grab a roller, and have at it."

My home was a work in progress. Since buying the place, it had sucked all my time and money, but it was nice having a few acres and being out of town. I saw enough of the school kids during term time. The last thing I wanted to do was see them more often when out of work. Screw that.

Being here meant I had some space, and while the house was much too big for one man, I made the most of spreading out and trying to make the place my own, one room at a time.

And apparently, the kitchen was next if Dan got his way.

I expected that would be the case.

2

DAN

Craig had chosen the perfect spot for fishing. Perched at the edge of the lake, the three of us snug in our camping chairs, I inhaled the fresh scent of gums caught in the gentle breeze.

This right here was what I'd been missing.

Between the birdsong and the gently lapping water, peace blanketed me, so much better than any comfort a duvet and a warm bed could offer.

While I could have made an effort to visit more regularly—it was only a couple of hours away rather than a million kilometres—visiting and then having to leave the place behind had become difficult.

Partly because things with my ex had been on rocky ground for a while, so knowing I'd be returning to a tense situation hadn't made me eager to leave.

A bigger part of that reason was to do with the two men beside me.

Craig had been my best mate forever, and maybe just by the luck of the draw, our friendship remained steady, surviving my many years away.

His more regular visits helped. That and his bloody-mindedness.

It was on Craig's last visit just three months ago that he'd called me out on staying away, reading me too well. It had taken his wake-up call for me to admit how miserable I was living in Brisbane. My job was okay, but it was just a job. I wasn't invested. And my social life had been non-existent.

Over the past year or so, it had been sheer stubbornness that kept me from moving back home. After the breakdown of my last and only semi-serious relationship, I'd learned my lesson that dating could screw up a decent friendship, as well as distance a whole social circle in the process.

There was something about being thirty-five and single, especially when the few friends who'd stuck with me after splitting with Duncan were loved up. I'd been set up on so many dates after my ex, I'd had to put more hours in at the gym to work off eating out so much.

But my heart hadn't been in it—the gym or the dating.

And honestly, meeting a guy hadn't filled me with anything but ill-ease.

I'd been exhausted by Duncan being a wanker and was so damn relieved that he'd never fully had my heart.

The reason for me never entirely giving my heart away was the man sitting at my right.

I side-eyed Ross as he cast off, a soft smile curving his mouth. Seemingly satisfied, he eased back in the canvas chair, tilted his head back, and closed his eyes.

Fuck, I could look at him all day.

Growing up, most of my memories were with the brothers, and there were only a handful of moments Ross took the title of an annoying younger sibling. Most of the time, he'd been cool and hung out with Craig and me.

His brother and I had always looked out for him, even more so when he'd come out—long before I'd figured myself out.

I didn't think any of us were surprised when Ross sat his family down at dinnertime one day—and me the day after—letting those he cared about know he was gay.

From how Craig told it, there'd been a collective sigh of relief—from how serious Ross had been in the moment, he'd pretty much terrified his family.

When Ross had told me, I'd nodded, nudged him, grabbed him in a headlock, and overbearingly demanded that once he started dating, any guy he was interested in had to be approved by Craig and me.

It wasn't until I was twenty-two and out one night with Craig that something clicked in my brain.

A legit epiphany had hit me hard, catching my breath. Unsurprisingly, it had been when Craig told me Ross had started dating some douche on his course.

"Pissed off" hadn't even come close to my reaction. The night had gone downhill from there, resulting in too much vodka and Craig dragging my arse back to the small apartment I was sharing with a guy from work.

When I'd spat my dummy out, telling him I didn't want to go home—and from memory that led to a tirade about Ross and his dick of a new boyfriend—Craig had called me out.

Him comparing me to a jealous boyfriend had fired me up, ready to argue back. But those deep brown eyes of his, the exact same shade as Ross's—

and knowing the shade of Ross's eye colour should have clued me in—had connected with mine, complete with raised brows.

That non-verbal "I call bullshit" had been all it took for me to slam my mouth shut and fall flat on my arse on the kerb.

My "Fuck, I'm gay" had resulted in Craig sitting at my side, arm pressed reassuringly against mine and sealing the deal with "No shit, and you have a big fat crush on my brother. That's gross, mate." His smirk had followed, as well as a more sober walk home, then twenty-four hours of "holy shit" conversation.

"Ouch. The fuck?" The elbow in my ribs jerked my attention to Craig. I shot him a glare. "You do that for?"

Silently, Craig lifted his brows high and gave a pointed look at his brother before shuttering his expression when I felt movement to my right. A quick glance in Ross's direction, and his gaze was on the two of us, a smirk on his lips.

I grinned at him, completely ignoring how Craig had caught me staring at Ross. Not that I could help it. The man had matured in the best of ways.

He wasn't as lean as he used to be, which I liked a lot. And at weekends, when he was in his rough and tumble clothes of jeans, plaid shirt, and when working at his place, an Akubra on his head, he looked especially fuckable. Much like he wore now, minus the plaid that was hidden by a sweater.

"You're going to scare the fish," Ross said.

"Right. Blame your brother for that. He can't keep his hands to himself."

Craig grunted. "Whatever. Just like someone can't keep their eyes to themselves."

My head whipped in his direction. He simply grinned at me. The arsehole.

"You know that doesn't make any sense, right?" Ross said, and I smirked at Craig, shooting him the finger.

"You see, Ross even agrees that you're full of shit."

"Ha. I did *not* say that," Ross said.

"May as well have, because it's true."

"It was an elbow, not hands," Craig defended. "And you," he grumbled, leaning forwards and eyeing his brother, "stop being so pedantic."

Ross raised a hand in defeat. "Just saying the two of you are noisy as hell."

The tug on my line drew my attention.

"You got something?" Ross asked.

"Looks like it." I held on to my rod and took my

time reeling it in, watching the rippling water as I drew in my catch.

"Five bucks it's a bass."

I didn't look at Craig as he placed his bet.

"Five on a golden perch," Ross added.

"I'll take the bet that it's neither."

"No way. Make your call. If no one wins, the kitty rolls over." Craig edged out of his chair a little, trying to get a better look.

"Fine," I grumbled.

A couple of minutes later and harder work than I remembered it being, I pulled out a saratoga. None of us won the wager. The fish was a good size too. I unhooked it and released it back into the water. These fish weren't for eating. It would be great to catch something to throw on the hot coals for lunch, though.

"You all set for starting your new job tomorrow?" Ross asked as we settled back down.

"Yeah." When I'd moved just over a week ago, I'd already secured the position at a local cabinetmaking place, specialising in making kitchens. I took last week off to get settled back into the swing of things and move my stuff into the small house I'd rented in town.

My parents had offered to let me stay at theirs,

and while they were away a lot travelling in their caravan, the thought of moving home wasn't on the top of my list of things to do.

"I know a couple of the guys working there from school." I removed my glasses and tugged my sweater off after I spoke, the morning winter sun having fully filled the sky, beating down on us. When I pulled it from my face, I glanced at Ross, my gaze zeroing in on the smattering of colour in his cheeks. His focus was dead ahead, his eyes wide, even obvious from his side profile.

I smirked, my ego doing a cheer, hoping to hell the pink in his cheeks was a reaction to my T-shirt riding high up on my chest when I'd tugged off the woollen sweater.

"Who's that?" Craig asked, drawing my attention away from his brother.

"Jared Healy and Bodhi Hanson."

"Huh. Jared was a few years above us, right?"

"Yeah, that's the one."

"His son goes to my school. Started Year 8 in January," Ross said.

My eyes widened in surprise. "Bloody hell, that makes me feel old." I shook my head, considering just how many people around our age were married and with kids. While I didn't know the number, it was sure to be a lot.

"Well, you're just about to flip over to thirty-six. That makes you closer to forty, right?"

Both my and Craig's heads whipped in Ross's direction so fast—and I imagined with matching expressions of "what the fuck did you just say?"—it was no wonder Ross broke into laughter.

"Jeez, be careful of such sudden movements. Bones get brittle when you get older."

My eyes narrowed, zeroing in on Ross's warm brown eyes, nothing but amusement dancing in their depths.

"You know what, Craig?" I said, not looking away from Ross.

"What's that?"

"I don't think a man's ever too old for a mid-morning swim."

Craig shifted immediately, popping onto his feet, his rod placed on the ground. I didn't remove my gaze from Ross. When his eyes widened, understanding registering, he jumped out of the chair, getting caught up in his rod.

"The pair of you can piss off," he shouted around his laughter. He detangled himself and shoved his rod onto the muddy bank, shoulders still shaking.

Before he could take a step back, I latched on to his wrist. His skin was warm under my hold. It wasn't the time to appreciate the softness of his hairs under my fingertips or even that of his skin.

"Oomph." The sound fell out of Ross when Craig wrapped his arms solidly around his chest. I ignored the flutter of frustration that I didn't think to go for that move. Though, having Ross pressed against me wouldn't have been the smartest decision.

"Grab his feet." Craig's grin filled his whole damn face, and I struggled to get a hold of Ross's feet, laughing too hard.

"Don't... you... dare, you fuckers." Ross's own laughter made each word an effort, each syllable sounding wheezy.

I latched onto his legs and hauled him up, struggling to see through my tears of laughter while Ross squirmed in my hold.

We manhandled him to the edge.

"If I touch that water, the both of you are joining me," Ross hollered, squirming some more.

I had absolute belief he was telling the truth. As a kid, he'd always found a way to take us down with him. Though, as a kid, I may not have put up too much of a fight, wanting to make sure the teasing went three ways.

When we shifted him close to the edge, Craig stopped, his smirk wide, gaze on me. "We throw him in, you know you're getting wet."

"You too. No chance you're escaping," I said.

"How about the pair of you just stop being dicks, put me down, and you two feel free to go for a swim?" Ross narrowed his eyes at me. He'd also given up the struggle. With his arms crossed over his chest, he almost seemed relaxed while Craig and I were busting our balls lifting him.

It was when he raised his brow in challenge, trying to call my bluff, that I shouted to Craig, "Now."

I caught the wide-eyed look on Ross's face, his mouth dropping open before Craig and I bounded into the lake together, throwing the three of us deep into the chilly water.

Craig's head broke free of the surface. Spluttering, he laughed, saying, "Holy shit, that's cold."

I could only snort in response, the frigid water capturing my ability to form words. While today was forecast a warm twenty-two degrees Celsius, perfect for a winter's day in Queensland, the nights were dropping to around three degrees, meaning the water was bloody cold.

"I think my dick's fallen off," Ross said through

chattering teeth, making me chuckle harder. Yet the three of us remained in the cold water, fully dressed and shivering, all of us having far too much fun freezing our arses off.

And me? I'd never been more certain that moving back was the right thing to do. And more than that, when Ross's gaze found my own, a smile aimed my way, I was convinced there could be something between us.

I'd waited over ten years for the chance and couldn't screw this up.

Not like last time.

Dating a friend in the past had bitten me on the butt and changed the dynamics of everything. I couldn't risk it again without being certain we were right for each other.

Time was on our side, though. I'd use it to reconnect with the man who'd had a piece of my heart for a hell of a long time.

3

ROSS

I'D READ ENOUGH NOVELS ACROSS SO MANY genres to understand how tension between two people was supposed to feel. I could recite poetry, analyse extended metaphors dedicated to the chemistry between people. Hell, I'd even dabbled at writing a couple of books—neither would ever see the light of day.

Even knowing all that didn't prepare me for Dan's return.

When I was a teenager, my crush seemed insignificant compared to now and how Dan filled my mind, and that was nothing compared to the time we spent together.

When he wasn't at work, we were together in some shape or form. While Craig was with us a lot too, Dan had talked me into modernising my kitchen in the past couple of months.

There was no hardship involved with spending practically every weekend with the man and multiple evenings too. Except I wasn't sure my heart could take it.

Every time I caught his gaze, the overactive organ tucked away beneath my rib cage would flip or do a straight-up somersault. And when he cast me that small secret smile that I'd convinced myself was just for me, a new circus performance would start up inside my body, my stomach joining in with the fun.

Between the acrobatics and the inevitable extended time of my right hand getting a workout, a strange level of exhaustion always seemed to nip at the edges of my being.

It was strange—and more extreme than the reaction of my eighteen-year-old self, or even the few times I'd seen Dan over the years. I could only put it down to being viscerally aware of every move the man took when he was close by.

And hell if I wasn't terrified that I was becoming obsessed, with just how often I watched him when we were together. But the man took my breath away as easily as a balloon might steal the breath from my lungs.

"You need something?"

"Huh?" My eyes focussed, and heat spread up my neck. I'd done it again. Dan stood next to the sink he'd just installed, sealant in hand and amusement flickering in his gaze.

"You seemed in another world. No fair if you were and I wasn't invited. That's just selfish, leaving me out like that."

I stood straight, leaning away from the door frame where I'd been perched, and rolled my eyes. "My imagination isn't all that good. You'd be better off sticking to a book."

As expected, he scrunched his nose. "Screw that. The movie, Ross. It's all about the movie."

I feigned indignation, this being a lifelong argument between us. "Don't even," I said. "The threat is still real. I'll sit you down and force you to listen to *Game of Thrones*."

He grinned in response, not seeming at all put out by that. Once again, my heart leaped, perhaps aiming for a trapeze. "Hanging out with you while you read to me for hours..." He trailed off and shrugged. "Worst. Punishment. Ever." A wink followed, the gesture having a direct link to the somersaults taking place inside my chest. The man was my very own ringmaster. And didn't that thought threaten to send me down a rabbit hole I'd struggle to come back from. "Wanna give me a hand?"

Yes, please. Instead of those words spilling out, I nodded. "Cupboard doors?"

"Yeah. You want to grab the screwdrivers and I'll bring in the doors?"

"On it."

Side by side, we worked together with idle chitchat, Dan telling me about a couple of his friends in Brisbane who'd recently married, and me sharing with him the details of my last trip overseas to Fiji.

"When's your next school holiday?"

I peered up at him. "Next month, the end of September."

He nodded before powering another screw into one of the hinges. "Any plans for trips away soon?"

"Not really. The world's a funny place at the moment, plus there's always something to do here, you know?"

Dan glanced over at me. "True that. What's next on your list?"

Easing off my knees, I stood, groaned, and angled back. A satisfying pop of my joints followed. Before I could respond to Dan's question, his "Fuck, I hate that sound," had me chuckling.

"But it feels so good."

His scrunched-up face looked somehow cute, despite his unshaven jaw and the streaks of dust on his cheeks. "But it sounds bloody awful."

I grinned and went back to his question. "As for the next job, I'm not sure yet. There's a few things I want to get done. Maybe start the firepit."

"Just in time for summer, huh." He quirked his brow.

With a roll of my eyes, I said, "If you don't want there to be a fire for toasting marshmallows, then keep up the snark."

"I wouldn't dare, not if marshmallows are on offer."

"Wise decision." I smirked before asking him about the training I knew he had next weekend. "Craig said you have a whole weekend thing going on, starting next Friday."

"Yeah. Should be a good laugh."

"A laugh... because that's important when fighting fires," I sassed.

Dan's grin was filled with mischief. "Humour is just the cream to go with a full-on weekend of training. The focus is bushfires."

"Summer's going to be here before we know it," I said. While our summer was also the rainy season, and now in August, we were already technically in fire season with the dry land, the last few fires around the state had sparked at the end of spring, beating the rains.

"And hopefully with it plenty of the wet stuff." He indicated towards the kitchen window. "It's looking dry out there."

"Makes me glad I only have the couple of cows and my annoying goats. Any more and I'd be buying in feed within the next couple of months, if we don't get a decent drop of rain." I followed Dan's focus when he returned his attention to the window and started laughing.

"Is there a reason why Benji's standing on Val's back?"

I craned my neck as I took a couple of quick steps closer to him, looking into the side paddock where my cows and goats were. Valkyrie, my Droughtmaster, was lounging in the sun, munching grass. She was the first cow I'd bought five years ago as a calf and had turned into a good breeder.

But she wasn't the brightest cow ever.

"Bloody hell. Benji's been a nightmare recently. Getting into everything." With a shake of my head, I wondered why the cow would allow a goat on its back in the first place. I took the few steps to the back door, Dan hot on my heels, and stepped outside.

Sun streaked across the veranda deck, which also needed some TLC. I ignored the long list of jobs buzzing in my brain and focussed on the vista, reminding myself why all the hard work was worth it.

The rolling hills of the valley were a sight I'd never tire of. The view was one of the main reasons why I couldn't resist the property, despite the rusty roof and the eighties-style everything.

The fence line of the paddock where the animals grazed was about ten metres or so away.

"Valkyrie," I hollered, "why are you letting the goat walk all over you?"

Dan snorted at my side, and my own laughter spilled out.

"You gonna tackle that?"

"Nope," I said. "There's no way I have the energy to deal with either of them."

"Probably wise." Dan's arm brushed against mine, and I soaked in his heat and touch. Being in his company was as easy as breathing, and just like air, I couldn't do without it. "Come on, let's finish these last couple of doors, and we'll grab a cold one."

"Good plan," I said with a nod and turned,

allowing myself an indulgent glance at how Dan's grey T-shirt pulled just so across his large chest. When I shifted my gaze up, our eyes caught, a small smile dancing on his lips. Like a kangaroo bounding over the road, facing an oncoming truck, I hesitated and dithered a little before a weird burst of laughter broke free. Only then did I hightail it back into the house.

Barely a moment passed before I thought I heard his quiet chuckle, but a quick glance in his direction showed his focus was back on the doors, and only his usual relaxed expression was evident.

Once we got stuck in, it only took about half an hour to finish off and ensure the doors aligned. We stepped back to see the finished units better, my grin quick and happy. "It looks amazing."

"Yeah. Good pick with the doors."

"They only look so great because of the counter-top." I wasn't blowing smoke up his backside either. Dan had managed to source some reclaimed timber and had spent time at work after hours preparing it.

I had no idea what sort of labour had gone into it. Still, the worktops were spectacular, all multi-coloured tones of oak, the imperfections on display to appreciate the natural timber.

Dan gave a slight nod of acknowledgement. It

was a sweet reaction. Though I hoped he knew just how talented he was. I did tell him often.

"So," Dan said, removing his specs and rubbing at one of his eyes, "we've earned ourselves that beer, right?"

"Definitely. And dinner. My treat for you being so talented."

When he angled to look at me, I mirrored the movement. "I could definitely be up for a meal."

"Great." My gaze darted around his face before trying to ease off the staring. "Early, about six do you?"

"That'll give me time to head to mine and get showered and changed."

"Cool. Let's pack away, and I'll book a table somewhere." While there weren't that many choices in town, it was still a good idea to book on a Saturday night.

An errant thought of reaching out to Craig and inviting him hit me. The question hovered on my lips about whether Dan wanted to ask him to come along. I held back, which took more effort than it should have. It wouldn't be the first time Dan and I headed out for a drink together. Dinner, though, was different, seemed more date-like.

Despite knowing it would be a shared meal

between friends, as well as an extra thank-you from me, I liked the idea of it just being just the two of us too much to make the offer.

"Sounds good."

By the time we got to Blossom Garden, the night had fully drawn in, the streetlamps leading the way. I'd driven over to Dan's, and we'd walked the couple of blocks into town to the Thai restaurant.

"I've never eaten here," Dan said from my side. "How long ago did it open?"

"A little before I came back to town, so maybe ten years."

I reached for the door and held it open, indicating for Dan to head on inside. He did so with a small uplift of his lips.

"Thanks."

We stepped into the warm space.

The restaurant was dimly lit, atmospheric almost. My eyes widened in surprise. The place hadn't been quite so romantic last time I'd come.

"Cosy." The dip in Dan's voice was enough to make me glance over. He playfully bounced his brows up and down, and ease settled in my chest.

"Low lighting helps the volume." My lips twitched at my bullshit explanation. "Stops people from being too loud and taking pictures of their food for Instagram."

Dan chuckled. "There go my plans for the night. I only came for the food presentation and photo ops."

I didn't have a chance to respond before the hostess appeared, asking if we'd booked. A moment later, we were settled around a small table on surprisingly comfortable chairs.

"Looks like they've refitted the place." The room, despite being large, managed to feel warm and intimate with an array of planters and dividers spread across it.

"It's been done out well."

I smirked at Dan, knowing that he looked at the quality of the fit-out when usually out and about. It was the nature of his job, just like I couldn't pass a bookstore without being drawn to the crisp or much-loved pages of a book.

"Let's hope the food's just as good as I remember and lives up to the new décor."

Looking at the menu, I saw so much on offer, it would be a struggle to decide. There were all my favourites, plus a few I'd never tried before.

"This is too hard," I grumbled.

"It all sounds amazing."

I transferred my focus to Dan, whose focus was on me.

"Wanna share a few starters and a couple of mains?"

"Yes, let's do that." My response was immediate, and with the soft smile directed my way, I was more than okay with my eagerness.

We talked through a few options, then made our order, pausing on drinks.

"If you want to drink, you can always stay over."

My attention shot to Dan, and I swallowed hard at the offer. It shouldn't be a big deal and probably wasn't in his eyes. He'd stayed over mine a few times now, but I'd never done so at his before.

"Uhm, yeah, that'd be great. Thanks."

"No worries." His gaze roamed my expression a beat before he turned to speak to the young waitress. While he did so, I racked my brains, pretty certain he only had the one bed.

There was always the couch, and I figured that's where I'd be sleeping. The thought of sharing with him, avoiding the invisible line in fear of snuggling up to the guy in my sleep, was a humiliation I wouldn't be able to get over.

"Ross?" Question filled his eyes when mine connected with his. "Drink?"

"Oh, sure. Sorry." A quick glance at the drinks menu, and I selected my beverage, handing the menus back to the waitress.

And then we were alone in our quiet little spot, just the right side of secluded to make this feel like a date. A voice from our right put a screeching halt to that, however.

"Dan Madison. I heard you were back in town."

The two of us turned to face the man who'd stopped when being led to a table. Awareness bit into my consciousness when my brain made sense of the face.

"Damn, is that Woolly too?" The man cackled, apparently pleased with the shorthand nickname he and his friends brandished in high school.

My right eye twitched as Jamie continued, seemingly oblivious to my clenched jaw and just what a dick he was. "Makes sense. You were always following Madison around even then." He turned his attention to Dan while I aimed to keep my agitation in check and not tell this dickhead to piss off. "I'm just visiting from Cairns. That's where I live now," he started, apparently thinking either of us gave a damn. "Mum said you moved back. What you doing with yourself?" Jamie shifted the waist of his jeans, his beer belly wobbling a little with it. While I was no slim Jim, this guy indulged a lot, and between his ill-fitting clothes and pockmarked skin, I took sadistic pleasure in knowing he wasn't aging well.

When Dan remained quiet for a beat, I moved my attention to him. With drawn brows, a look of distaste seemed at war with bemusement on his face. "Jamie, right?" he settled on, his eyes darting quickly to me. I attempted to smooth over my expression, but I expected I failed, since the bemusement dropped away. With his eyes back on the man who couldn't read a room and wouldn't know tension if it hit him square in the face, Dan asked, "Woolly? What's that about?"

Jamie chuckled while I froze. Pulling myself back together as quickly as possible, I opened my mouth to speak but was beaten to the punch by Jamie, saying, with a laugh that suggested we were in cahoots, "Just something me and Nick used to call *Rochelle* here back in the day."

Heat slammed into me, right alongside indignation and an almighty what the fuck! "They couldn't help with the lame attempt at nicknames." I quirked my right brow high, looking directly at Jamie as I spoke. "Neither of them was particularly smart," I said with a butter-wouldn't-melt smile. Attempting to emasculate me when I was a kid was one thing; now I was a man, Jamie could go fuck himself.

"I was only being—"

"A prick?" My smile remained true, my eye contact unwavering as I spoke.

"Do I want to know about 'Woolly?'" Dan's voice held a thread of steel beneath what seemed to be carefully placed amusement. A quick look at the man sitting opposite me, and I read his expression clearly.

He was unimpressed and wanted this dipshit gone as much as I did.

Taking control of this narrative, I answered, "That was from another bank of genius nicknames gifted to me. Woolly woofter, rhymes with poofter, right, Jamie?" I rolled my eyes at the man. "Unoriginal Homophobic Slurs 101," I said, the words pouring out. I didn't give myself time to marvel at how different my reaction was now to a couple of months back when Craig and Dan had innocently mentioned the pitiful excuse of a man before me. All I knew was I was on a roll, and my snark was fast and strong. "Hey, it sounds like a book title. You should get together with some of your old pals, Jamie, give it a whirl. There's even software that'll help you out with spelling."

As soon as I was finished, I looked away. My heart thickened in my throat, my adrenalin already threatening to crash.

I had no idea what had come over me, nor could I get a grasp on how I felt about the whole exchange, but I zoned out the conversation around me, taking a relieved swig of my drink when it magically appeared before me.

"Hey."

Somehow the softness of that one word cut through the pounding in my ears. Lifting my head, I locked eyes with Dan. Worry pinched his brows, and I attempted a shaky smile. Knowing how forced it was, I cracked my neck from side to side and tried to relax my shoulders.

Shock at the past few minutes had me breaking out into a chuckle, bemused at the whole exchange. "So, that just happened."

Rather than laughing with me, Dan's brows dipped further. "You want to get out of here?"

A quick scan of the room, and I didn't see Jamie anywhere.

"He and his wife left," Dan said.

"Shit." My cheeks heated, all too aware I'd made a spectacle of myself.

"No." He shook his head, reading my reaction. "I think we were all surprised, but the guy had it coming. He could have simply said hi and walked away, ignoring the memory of the bullshit he threw at you years ago, but he didn't. The wanker instead made a joke of it. That shit's not okay."

I absorbed his words, clutched on to the thread of praise I heard in his voice. That and the fact he didn't think I'd made an idiot of myself helped me release a heavy breath.

"I just got started, you know? The words, they just spilled out and kept going."

When his frown eased away, and amusement filled his gaze, I grinned. His mouth twitched in response. "I kinda got that."

I laughed, the sound loud in the quiet restaurant. It took me a moment to control myself, enjoying the sensation of feeling safe and appreciated in Dan's company. And more than that, feeling fucking victorious in my smack down.

"You good?"

"Surprisingly, yeah."

"Perfect, 'cause the food over there I think is ours, and after those mad few minutes, I'm starving." He lifted his beer bottle and tipped the neck out to me. I tapped mine to it. "Cheers to us and cutting through homophobia, one idiot at a time." He followed up with a wink, and I struggled to swallow my beer, my skin flushed and tingly, and wishing we could have celebrated with a proper date and a kiss.

By the time we ambled back to Dan's, exhaustion beat hard at me. The food coma didn't help, but I was still wired from the exchange with Jamie.

"Thanks again for the meal." Dan's voice echoed in the quiet night. Until then, only the sound of cicadas and the occasional car engine in the distance had filled the air.

"No worries. I owe you more than one with all the work you've been doing, which I really appreciate, in case I hadn't told you."

Dan chuckled. "You may have already said a time or five."

The side of my mouth quirked up as we carried on in companionable silence. I appreciated the ease of Dan's company.

Focusing ahead on the moonlight spilling between the frangipanis lining the pavement, I hummed in contentment. It would be awesome if this was the norm, a part of our life, but I could read

Dan well enough to know he wasn't looking at anything beyond friendship.

There was a distance between us, miniscule, but it was there all the same. Sure, there was an occasional look or even mild flirtation, but there were similar levels of friendliness between Dan and a couple of our friends, so nothing had changed.

For the moment, though, I was content in getting to know Dan all over again.

The past few months we'd spent a good portion of our days and evenings together. Regardless of how my body practically sizzled when he was close, I could keep that emotion at bay and luxuriate in his company.

"You planning on staying the night?" Dan asked when we arrived outside his house.

"If that's okay?" I asked. After the confrontation with Jamie, I'd had more to drink than was safe to drive. The walk had helped clear my head, but a breathalyser would have me over the limit.

"Course. You can even test out the new bed in the spare room."

When a nugget of disappointment bloomed in my chest, I batted it away. "Awesome. When did you get that?"

"It was delivered a couple of weeks ago. Just

thought I should make an effort in case someone needs to stop by." Unlocking the door, he gestured me ahead.

The rental property was a relatively plain two-bedroom low-set house, but it was convenient for his work and had a small garage and carport.

"You planning on having visitors?" I asked, heading straight into the kitchen so I could grab a drink of water. Once at the tap, I glanced over to Dan. "You want water too?"

He nodded. "There's cold water in the fridge, though, in the filter jug."

I turned to the fridge and pulled it out as Dan collected a couple of glasses.

"And as for visitors, you're here, aren't you?"

I leaned against the countertop. "Not sure I count. What about your friends in Brissy?"

He scrunched his nose and passed me a full glass of water. I took it and followed him into the sparse sitting room. It wasn't a surprise the place didn't exactly look lived in, considering where he spent most of his time. The sliver of guilt cutting through me took me by surprise. Had I monopolised his time so much he hadn't even settled in properly?

My gaze flicked to his when he sank into the cushions of his dark blue sofa.

"Maybe. Things were, I don't know... a bit weird in Brissy before I left."

My brows shot to my hairline. Since being back, Dan had barely mentioned Brisbane or his time there. While I knew about his break-up, it had also happened a while before he'd returned to town. Other than that, I'd assumed he'd been having a good time.

It had only been when Craig had told me Dan was returning that I asked a half-hearted why. Not truly caring why he was coming back, just that he was.

Figuring that made me a shit friend, disappointment ached in my chest.

A grimace formed on my face. "I'm sorry. I didn't realise. I just thought.... Actually, I don't even know what I thought the reason was for you heading back north. I was too caught up in being happy that you were," I admitted, ignoring the burn in my cheeks.

Dan's smile was soft. "You've nothing to be sorry about. I haven't offered up any information, wasn't really keen to talk about it."

I stilled at his words, holding my breath for a beat. "Shit, did something bad happen?" The thought that he hurt brought forth a wave of unexpected emotion. It had been a night of it, apparently.

But my bullshit run-in with a high school bully was nothing to the concern thrumming in my veins at the possibility of Dan not being okay.

When he shook his head, I expelled a heavy breath. Despite the line etched between his brows, he formed a smile. "No... well, not physically. Perhaps a bit hurt there for a while."

"Because of Duncan?"

Removing his glasses, Dan rubbed at his eyes and placed his specs on the armrest. "Well, he didn't help."

In all honesty, I didn't know much about his past relationship. I hadn't met the guy. All Craig had told me was Duncan was "all right." Not the most glowing or helpful of reports. Beyond them being together for a couple of years, that was the extent of my knowledge.

My title as crap friend seemed secure, but self-preservation was one heck of a motivator.

I remained quiet, not sure what to ask or say, hoping he'd continue so I could understand Dan and his past better.

After a gulp of water, his expression softened when he directed it at me. "Duncan could be... difficult."

"Okay?" I dragged the word out, immediately

wondering why they'd been together for so long if that was the case.

"We were friends, actually, for a couple of years before we sort of, I don't know, fell into a relationship. I met him originally through a guy at work. Duncan's his cousin. We hung out, and I soon joined his group of friends. They're who I hung out with most of the time, but when things didn't work out between me and Duncan, our... *his* friends sort of closed ranks."

"What, like all of them?"

"Not quite, there's Mish and Lee, who I still saw, and Ian and his partner, Phil, but everyone else made it clear it would be awkward since they were friends with Duncan."

My expression hardened. "It sounds like you're better off without them anyway, if they can just do that." What I really wanted to do was call them all insignificant arseholes, not worthy of his time or energy, and say I wished he'd come home sooner. I kept my mouth shut, not needing Dan to see just how riled up the idea of him being shut out and lonely made me.

"So yeah, your brother told me to come home, and it didn't take too much convincing."

"Good. You belong here."

His gaze hit mine. "Yeah. That's what I think too."

A crackle of tension grew, and I swallowed hard. What I wouldn't give to lean in and eat up the distance between us, finally pressing my mouth to his. I shifted a little, my body getting on board and liking that idea.

"It was a hell of a lesson," he said, his mouth twisting as he worried his lower lip.

Dan's words pulled me up short. I straightened, my back becoming ramrod straight. "What was?"

"Getting involved with a friend."

The punch to my chest had me catching my breath. My heart squeezed tightly as his words bounced around my brain. I lowered my head, needing to look away, too terrified my pain would be front and centre for him to see. I struggled as my throat swelled with emotion, choking down my distress at hearing his words and the truth in them.

When I didn't respond, he cleared his throat. "You okay?"

"Yeah, sure," I croaked. "Just tired. Perhaps we should go to sleep?" The need for space brought me to my feet.

"Sure. You need anything?"

"Nope," I answered a little robotically and then forced myself to look at him.

Confusion swam in the depths of his tawny eyes.

And that right there told me all I needed to know. His innocent, honest words were shared with no idea of how they'd impact me. The concern was for my reaction, me closing down, and that was all on me.

I managed a smile, trying to make it as sincere as possible. "Thanks for tonight. I'll see you in the morning."

Before he could respond, I left the sitting room, making my way to the bedroom. Each step I took, the ache in my heart became more pronounced.

Things had to change. I needed to try to let go. It was the only way our friendship—and my heart—could survive.

4

———

DAN

WE SAT AROUND ROSS'S NEW FIREPIT, KEEPING warm from the dip in temperature since the sun dropped about an hour earlier. While spring was well and truly here with the days warming up and the sun dipping a little later, the evenings still had a small bite.

We'd also had a couple of weeks of much-needed rain, the only reason we could actually give Ross's new firepit a test drive.

"Throw the bag."

I leaned over and picked up the giant bag of marshmallows, checked the clip was on, and then launched it at Craig.

He snatched the bag out of the air with a "Thanks" and put a giant marshmallow on his camp fork. Those had been my genius idea rather than relying on twigs.

There was nothing worse than enjoying a gooey marshmallow to only have to start picking splinters out of your mouth.

For the past week, I'd been heading to Ross's after work and helping him with his firepit. He'd told me more than once I didn't have to stop by every day, but screw that. Spending time with him had become one of my favourite things, despite the past few weeks not seeing him quite as often. But as soon as his school holiday had arrived, I'd put up my hand to help with the firepit he planned to make. Finally spending a bit of time with him was too good of an opportunity to miss.

Me hanging out with Ross had been noticed by pretty much everyone in our small circle of friends. It made me uneasy, but Ross and I weren't dating, so I had nothing to worry about.

Craig had spent more time with one of Ross's work friends, Alec, a good guy. When I'd first met the man, there had been a twinge of something very close to jealousy when I realised how often he and Ross hung out. But apparently, that was before I returned and "stole" him away.

I'd perhaps grinned, a little too happy at that.

Plus, there was the reassurance the guy was straight, and from hearing some of the stories he and Craig had shared since I'd been home, there was no questioning the legitimacy of that.

A loud yawn tore out of me, and I stretched my arms and shook my head.

"Keeping you up?" Craig asked.

I yawned again. "All good. Just relaxing."

"I said you were taking on too much last week, working full days, then here, and all bloody day today."

My eyes shot open wide at the bite in Ross's words, and I frowned in his direction.

Even in the shadows of the dancing flames, I could see his frustration, and I had little doubt guilt was the reason behind that.

"Don't be daft. It's fine. I said I'd help, so I did."

"But you look halfway ready for bed already."

I shrugged. "Stop stressing over it. It's not like it was a hardship coming and giving you a hand. Plus, you gave me a sweet deal."

Craig choking on his beer drew both of our attention in his direction. He sat up, coughing and wheezing, hand over his mouth. "Fuck," he spluttered.

"What's a matter with you?" I eyed him speculatively to make sure he could take a breath so wouldn't keel over, but also wondering what—

As soon as I started with that train of thought, I figured out his reaction. "*Dinners*. Your brother *fed* me."

That just got me a quirked brow in return, and I rolled my eyes at him. Glancing away, my attention moved to Ross. He was shaking his head at his brother, so I had little doubt he'd caught up.

"Stop worrying about what happens between me and Dan and focus on the mess of women you keep getting yourself involved in."

I would have laughed at the incredulity in Craig's "What? What have you heard?" if my brain wasn't caught on Ross's words. Did he want something to happen? Was he feeling this connection as much as I was... beyond that of friendship?

My mind continued to question every touch, every smile, every lingering glance, but fuck, I had to be sure. When I'd come back to town, I'd promised myself time to build up to something, wanting to make sure my attraction to Ross wasn't based on the idea or fantasy of him.

We'd changed so much over the years, and I refused to risk what we had if I screwed up somehow and made things awkward as fuck.

"He's not even listening," Craig said, breaking me out of my thoughts. I did manage to latch on to his words and the amusement evident in his tone. The arsehat knew exactly why I'd drifted off.

I flipped Craig off and looked at Ross. He shifted his attention away for a beat before returning his focus back on me. "I was saying Mum's already talking about Christmas plans. Are your folks around then, or are you coming over to Mum and Dad's?"

Affection unfurled in my stomach that he wasn't simply extending an invite but laying out the expectation I'd be joining him and his family should my parents not be around.

The last two Christmases had been spent in Brisbane. The one before that in Sydney when I'd headed out and spent it with my parents.

"Your folks' place," I answered immediately. "Not sure when my parents are heading back again. I need to reach out to them and check out their plans. I don't think they're here for Christmas."

"Well, if they end up being here, they can come too."

"Thanks, I'll let them know." I allowed my glance to linger a fraction longer than appropriate before the bag of marshmallows landed in my lap. I grunted and sent Craig an incredulous look. The bastard mimicked wiping drool off his mouth before he cracked up laughing at himself.

"Did you agree to go on that date?"

Craig's question ripped through the air. My head whipped in his direction. While I figured as much, his focus on his brother hit me hard. He couldn't have been asking me that question, since there was no date in sight.

Scowling, I flicked my attention to Ross.

The pointed look he sent to Craig didn't escape me. My breath caught in my throat, and while desperate to ask a question, I wasn't sure which one to settle on or if I wanted to know the answer.

Ross saved me from potentially embarrassing myself when he shook his head, startled eyes wide open. "No," he confirmed. That one word sent a rush of relief into me, but that was immediately followed by wondering why I didn't know what they were talking about.

"I'm confused. Alec said you'd agreed and exchanged numbers." Craig frowned at his brother.

Ross shrugged. "I changed my mind."

It was impossible not to ask. "What date?"

Ross's shoulders turned rigid before he seemed to forcefully relax them. "Nothing. There's no date."

My eyebrows furrowed. "Okay, but someone

asked you?" Curiosity battled it out with jealousy. Not quite sure which was winning, I attempted to keep my tone natural. There wasn't a chance I'd look at Craig, though. The man knew too much, and this conversation right here was because of his shit-stirring. I was fully aware of that and knew it was time I had it out with him. He needed to back off, regardless of whether his intentions were good or not.

"Just a guy who I see at the bar occasionally."

I latched on to the inside of my cheeks, trying to stop the third-degree questions burning my tongue. "Oh, okay." I wondered if the guy was good-looking and nice. I also wondered why Ross had changed his mind.

I hesitated, questioning whether I'd have asked another friend those questions if I wasn't so heavily invested in their answers. My forced smile slipped, knowing if this was about Craig, I'd be asking all sorts of questions and probably giving him shit.

I just didn't have it in me to play that card.

"Alec said Carl was hot." There went Craig again. I shot him the stink eye, trying my hardest to shut him down.

Needing to try to change tacks, I asked, "Since when does Alec think men are hot?"

Craig shrugged. "I dunno. Ask him. I think we

can all acknowledge when someone is fit or not, right?"

My mouth twitched. "Look at you not getting caught up in toxic masculinity or some shit. I'm so proud of you."

He snorted, following with a lopsided smile. "I live for your praise and approval," he deadpanned, making us all laugh.

I followed the sound of Ross's chuckle. The gleam in his eyes was genuine and a sharp difference to a few moments ago. Taking in the sight of him, I breathed a little easier. Just maybe his lack of interest in this Carl was more than the man not being his type or something.

He flashed his bright smile at me, one I'd missed from not spending as much time with the man.

Maybe his lack of interest was more to do with me.

A bloke could dream.

THE NEXT DAY, CRAIG AND I MET UP FOR AN afternoon drink. It had been a while since just the two of us caught up, plus I really did need to talk to him about his brother.

"You wanna tell me why you really asked to see my pretty face?" The corners of his eyes crinkled as he spoke. I should have known he'd figure out I wanted to talk to him.

"Ross."

He lifted an eyebrow and his chin, indicating I should carry on.

"I need you to stop stirring."

He eased back in his chair and tilted his head. "What do you mean?"

"Seriously?"

"Yeah, seriously."

"You saying things like you did yesterday, looking at getting a reaction out of me."

He bobbed his head slowly. "And you think that's stirring and not giving you the gentle nudge you so clearly need."

I rubbed my neck and huffed out a breath. "Yeah, it's stirring." He made to speak, but I shook my head, saying, "Look, I get it."

"You do? 'Cause as far as I can see, you don't get anything." Frustration laced his words, taking me by surprise.

"And what's that supposed to mean?"

"Since being back, it's like Ross is your sun." He waved me off when my lips twitched at the poetry of his words. "You gravitate around him or some shit."

I froze, my desire to take the piss out of him slipping as I wondered if I was that obvious and if that was a bad thing. Was he saying I needed to back off? That I was too much up in Ross's business?

"Fuck, I can see your mind whirling there. Just stop it. Whatever you're thinking that's bad, just dismiss it, okay?"

My breath quickened despite his words, and warmth flushed across my skin. I was so not used to reacting this way, let alone talking about this sort of thing with anyone.

"All I'm saying is if you want something to happen, you need to do something about it. If not, move on and let him look elsewhere."

"You mean this Carl guy?" Bitterness crept into my tone.

There was nothing casual about Craig's shrug. Concern radiated off the guy. "All I know is that Ross is holding out for something."

"Me?" Heat suffused me.

He shook his head. "I don't know. He's never said anything to me, but he's a good man."

"I know he his."

"And that's why you either need to step up or let

him go. You're hurting yourself, and probably him, by dragging this out."

His words were a punch to the gut, but perhaps I needed to hear them. While my intentions had absolutely been good, me holding out to be sure our friendship could survive wasn't fair on either of us, and that was only assuming Ross was actually interested.

The thing was, me being too chickenshit to come out and ask him probably meant I didn't deserve a shot at all. And if things didn't work out and it screwed up my relationship with Craig as well, then I'd be doubly screwed over.

I sighed, not quite sure what I was supposed to do, but I knew what I should do. And fuck if I didn't hate having to be a good guy.

5

———

ROSS

Between the busiest time of year at school and my promise to myself to not throw myself at Dan, I hadn't seen the man in three weeks.

I should have been happy that there was some separation between us.

But I wasn't.

At all.

Not seeing Dan, one of my closest friends, especially after spending so much time with him, felt like I was wading through my days.

It was no surprise I regretted pulling away in the first place, but since he'd ended up helping with the firepit over the September break, I'd sort of pushed my original promise aside. We'd easily fallen back into hanging out, our routine of seeing each other practically every day no hardship.

But since then, nothing.

I'd given in last weekend to see if he wanted to come for a fish, but he'd said he already had plans. Since Craig had gone fishing with me, my imagination had taken on a mind of its own, wondering if he'd gone on a date. I'd even asked Craig what Dan was up to, and he'd shrugged noncommittally, which soured my mood something fierce.

The whole situation was pissing me off and getting me down.

Feeling needy was not a look I wore well. I hated it, in fact.

Needing a distraction, I went in search of Alec. The school day hadn't long finished, so I hoped he was still in the PE office and hadn't left. The department was notorious for never answering their phone, so I didn't waste my time getting someone to pick up.

The sound of a ball slapping against the floor greeted me as I stepped into the large sports hall. Alec dribbled a basketball, moved a few paces, and took a shot. It sank in without touching the sides.

"Whoop!" I hollered.

His head flicked in my direction, and he grinned. "Coming to work up a sweat?"

The wrinkling of my nose was automatic. Sports and I were not friends. "That'd be a hard pass."

"What? You want a hard pass... of this ball?"

"I'd prefer a beer."

He stopped bouncing the ball immediately and bobbed his head. "A beer is a good alternative. You wanna meet me there or wait for me? I need maybe ten minutes."

"I can wait. I need to turn the computers off in the library."

"Sweet," he said, releasing the ball and sinking it.

"Leave the ball here!" I called out as I turned to leave.

"I bet that's not what you usually say to the guys!"

My chuckle joined his own as I headed back to the library.

Twenty minutes later, we were armed with drinks and seated in a quieter section of the pub. It wasn't busy, since it was a Tuesday.

Quiet country music played in the background but was inoffensive enough to almost blend in with the clink of glasses and low chatter.

Ben, the owner, looked to be stocking the spirits, while his wife, Lynnie, chatted to a couple of women. The other handful of patrons were keeping to themselves. It was one of the reasons why I liked this place so much. It was friendly without people being all up in your business.

"You had a decent day?"

"Yeah, not too bad," I answered. "Same old, you know? Busy with sorting all of the assignments."

"Urgh. Don't remind me. Scanning all of this shit in to send off to the exam board is a ball ache. I can't wait till it's all done and the countdown to the summer holiday is on."

"Not long and Year 12s will be out of here."

Relief flooded Alec's features. "I can't wait. They're all so bloody stressed, and we're all under the pump. Poor buggers."

He wasn't wrong.

The summer holidays would be with us before we knew it. At least come Christmas, I'd actually get to spend some time with Dan, I thought humourlessly. He'd already agreed, and I couldn't see him changing his mind. "You made plans for Christmas?"

"Bali for five weeks."

My brows shot up. "And I'm only hearing about this now?"

Alec chortled. "Literally just sorted it this weekend. Trevor talked me into it."

Understanding registered. I'd met his younger

brother a couple of times when he'd visited town. He was a force of nature and seemed to talk Alec into a lot of things. "Brilliant. Just the two of you?"

"Mainly." He took a swig of his drink and then exhaled heavily enough it caught my attention. "A couple of his friends are flying out for, I think, one week. And Mum and Dad are going to be over for Christmas, maybe the New Year."

I squinted a little in his direction, trying to get a better read on his reaction. Coming up short, I said, "You make it sound like that's an issue."

The curious flush in his cheeks got my attention.

"Spit it out."

He fidgeted a little, something I'd never seen him do before. Finally, after what seemed like a lifetime, he said, "One of his friends has a bit of a thing for me."

Somehow I held back my snort, immediately making the comparison with me having a thing for one of my friends.

"And you don't like her?"

"Him."

My brows lifted. "Huh. And he knows you're straight?" I tilted my head, curiosity burning through me.

"Yeah, he knows, and he's a good guy. I just feel awkward."

I frowned. "Because he's a man?"

He shook his head, gaze locking on mine. "It's not even that. It's that I like him... as a friend," he clarified. "But hanging out with him makes me feel like shit because I'm worried about leading him on."

Warmth filled my heart to such an extreme, I was sure it'd burst.

"Fuck, you're a good guy."

A sheepish smile lifted his lips, and he shrugged. "I try." The follow-up wink he sent me eased the seriousness of the moment, and I chuckled.

The story he shared was so similar to my own that it made me pause.

Did Dan know how I felt about him and had tried to let me down gently? "Holy shit," I said aloud.

"What?"

"Nothing. Just thought of something I forgot to do," I bullshitted. My brain fired all over the place. When Dan had told me dating friends was a lesson learned, he'd been doing it then—letting me down gently—followed by distancing himself the past few weeks.

"You know, you're a bloody genius at times," I said, feeling better that understanding finally was in my grasp. While it did nothing to ease my mortification and the hurt bubbling in my gut, at least now I knew what was likely going through Dan's mind.

Why he'd distanced himself.

The knowledge meant I could focus on being his friend and finding ways to reassure him that his friendship was more important than anything else between us.

I forced my heart into a box, padlocking it up tight, and promised myself there'd be a time I'd let it out again. But for now, reconnecting with Dan as friends would be my new mission.

"I'm not taking no for an answer."

Armed with takeout from the Thai place we'd eaten at a while back, I stood at Dan's door, wafting the bag in front of me so he'd be hit with the delicious scent.

"And why would I say no if you've brought me food?" He quirked his brow at me and directed at me that familiar grin that made my knees weak.

"Uh-huh." It was all I offered, knowing we were as bad as each other, dancing around my feelings for him. It was time we stopped. I missed him too much to give him up.

He stepped to the side, letting me in. "You want beer?"

"That'd be great." I'd have just the one with my meal, meaning I'd be fine to drive home. Tonight was about reconnecting and setting the record straight. I balked at my thoughts, calling bullshit, as there wasn't a chance I'd be laying my feelings bare before him—especially as I expected it was my feelings that had made him run in the first place.

With that in mind, tonight's mission was reaffirming we were friends and securing that friendship with him was doable and important.

Perhaps my New Year's resolution could be to move on—but meaning it this time. That would give me a few weeks to let go properly and commit.

"So what brought this on?" Dan asked as he tugged out a couple of plates while I collected the utensils.

I sat down and started divvying up the food. "It feels like forever since we caught up. Just making sure you're still here and haven't done a runner back to Brissy or something."

He angled to look at me as I spoke, his eyes guarded, though I could have easily been interpreting reactions that weren't there. "No chance of that," he said after a beat.

"Good job too. Craig wouldn't take too much convincing to hold you hostage, perhaps sabotage your ute or something." I kept my tone light, just as it ought to be, focusing on setting the tone for how our friendship always had been.

His light snort as he picked up a forkful of food eased some of the ache in my chest.

"Craig doesn't seem to need much convincing about anything."

"You see what happens when you're not around? He needs retraining and reining in," I joked.

His lips twitched before he took a mouthful of food. The hum of appreciation was difficult to ignore, the sound joyous and seductive. I urged the throb in my pants to go away, pleading with it to calm down, reminding myself that friends didn't get a twinge from friends making happy sounds.

"Thanks for this," he said after we ate in silence. "I was still contemplating what to cook."

"No worries." I offered a casual shrug. "You been busy today?"

"A little. I went round Mum and Dad's this morning and ran the mower around."

"They have grass?" My brows jolted skyward,

genuinely surprised. Most of town and the neighbouring properties surrounding it were dry. There were still occasional hints of green closer to the drying creeks, but I'd seen several veils of dust created by a couple of houses I'd passed by attempting to mow.

"Yeah, but only because it's been five weeks since it was last mowed. I can't imagine it needing cutting again until the rain comes."

"Craig said you're all on bushfire watch." Worry gnawed at me and had done since Craig told me there'd been an alert change. It didn't help that there'd been a couple of news reports early last week about localised bushfires in north New South Wales. While that was several hours away, any mention of fires on the east coast always had the same effect on me.

"Yeah. I headed to the station earlier just to do a check of equipment."

I willed the thumping of my heart to settle, knowing I was overreacting. But I was more than aware that Dan hadn't tackled a fire since re-joining the rural fire brigade. It didn't matter that he had when he was younger. Lots of years had passed by since then.

"You okay about it all?" When his brows

furrowed, I clarified, "If you're called out. I know it's been some time."

The smile he sent my way made my heart flip. I sighed inwardly, frustrated I couldn't control my feelings. It just made me more determined to ensure outwardly, I was nothing but friendly, with no love-heart eyes in sight. Nor a hard-on that would give me away.

"Yeah. I know it's been a few years, but not a lot has changed. Those four years I did before I left for Brissy left their mark. And I like to think now I'm not quite as gung-ho."

I chuckled. "Well, that's a relief. You don't need to go all Rambo on a job."

"Not even if a red bandana would look awesome?"

"Even then." I punctuated my words with an eye-roll.

"Speaking of Rambo, you wanna watch a movie or something? Finish this in the sitting room?" He gestured towards the beer and half-eaten food.

"Sure. I think the latest *Rambo* movie is on Netflix, maybe. If not one of the other million apps you pay for."

His laughter was loud. "Right. I was determined

not to get trapped with a Foxtel subscription or bill, yet I now pay for at least six TV apps."

"Tell me about it. I keep going to cancel a couple and then get dragged into a new TV show."

"Hook, line, and sinker, right?"

"Yes! I'm sure they all add up to more than bloody Foxtel now," I grumbled, carrying my food and drink into the sitting room.

"The hardships of life, huh!"

"Yeah, yeah, I know. I'm a terrible person." I pulled a face at him, earning me a laugh.

We settled down, and Dan searched for the latest *Rambo* movie. I relaxed against the comfortable cushion and smiled. While I hadn't perfected my reaction or my longing quite yet, this—the hanging out, the chilling—I could do.

Connecting with Dan was worth the discomfort of keeping my feelings buried, and I could still make that commitment for a New Year's resolution.

I could definitely do this.

6

———

DAN

Since being back in town, it was times like these when I really questioned my good judgment. When I lived in the city, everything followed a set routine, especially last year. It was a time of work, gym, beer, and sleep. Rinse and repeat.

There was stability in living in the city.

Here on the Sunshine Coast hinterland, with the breeze picking up, the heat pressing against my skin, and smoke in the air, it was as far from routine or ordinary.

Everything changed so fast.

Between the past few weeks of no rain, the scorching heat, and not enough rural firefighters like myself on the ground, exhaustion was my new best friend or worst enemy—I hadn't quite decided. All I knew was functioning on barely any sleep and trying to balance my day job with my volunteer firefighting work meant I was running on fumes.

But we all were, and knowing we weren't getting smashed like many of our neighbouring regions simply made me feel guilty, especially as I was so relieved.

"You good?"

The sound of Craig's voice had me stretching my neck and glancing up. He looked like how I felt. His soot-covered face would take a good scrub or five in the shower, and I expected even showering would be an effort considering the sleep evident in his eyes.

"Yeah." I bobbed my head and reached for the passenger door.

We'd been out for only five hours or so on a small blaze, having taken over from a crew who'd been battling with the damn thing seven hours or so by the time Craig and I got there.

Small.

I snorted in my head at the word. "Small" took twelve hours and eight crew members. It had been like that for the past twelve days. This summer had been out of control.

I'd only talked to Ross a couple of weeks or so back about my previous stint as a rural firefighter. I'd joined as soon as I was old enough, so at sixteen with my parents' permission, and had done so for the four years before I left, seeking a different life.

I'd fought my fair share of fires back then, but nothing like the fires we, and the east coast at large, were dealing with today.

It seriously was so different.

"You want to pick up a takeaway on the way back?" Craig asked, starting the engine now he'd stripped out of his uniform, having dumped it in the tray of his ute.

"Noodles would be good and quick." My stomach rumbled as if on cue.

He nodded, took a quick look at his phone, and smiled before putting his Toyota in gear and pulling away. "Ross messaged."

My stomach flipped and fluttered at the mention of his brother. "Yeah?" Unsure if my voice was as neutral as I attempted or not, I glanced out the window, gaze on the smoky air, making dusk appear even darker.

"He made lasagne for us both, said he's already dropped it off."

I smiled at Ross's thoughtfulness.

He was always doing stuff like that, even more so over the past couple of weeks, with the call-outs. Being a school librarian meant he was off work since it was the school holidays. When I'd told him he didn't need to go to so much trouble, he'd rolled his eyes in that way he did when a little embarrassed and a bit annoyed while trying to not make a big deal out of it. The conversation had ended with him telling me to rack off, and he'd help out however he could, and I needed to suck it up.

If only he'd known how *that* comment had brought so many illicit thoughts to my mind.

Ross was impossible to be around. Well, if impossible meant I was always finding an excuse to spend time with the guy, even though I'd promised myself and Craig I'd back off. It was more to do with me finding it *impossible* to be around him while ignoring how he made me feel. How he made my heart beat fast. How, over the past few months, I was finding it more and more difficult—yeah, almost impossible—to make a move without ruining everything. The pull to see if there was something more between us rode me hard every damn day.

Six months since being home and being reminded just how fucking perfect he was, and I was still holding back. That dread of a destroyed friendship remained a heavy weight pressing against my chest that I just couldn't get past.

"You listening?"

"Huh?"

Craig chuckled. "I'm not even going to ask what's got you so distracted."

The bastard knew.

I didn't make a secret about still enjoying Ross's company, finding excuses to help him out on his small property. But Craig hadn't pushed the discussion we'd had a couple of months back either. I expected that was because he knew me well enough to understand how much I cared for his brother. It didn't matter that I hadn't come out and said the words, well, not since I'd first come out. To this day, even after I'd left town for a few years, Craig read me well.

"What did I miss?" There was no point in pretending I'd been listening.

He snorted a laugh. "Just checking you were good with lasagne. Ross has put the container in the outdoor fridge on your back veranda for you."

"Lasagne's great." It seriously was.

While Ross wasn't the best of cooks, he didn't screw up three dishes—lasagne, chilli, and stew. He could ply me with those all he wanted, especially after eight hours at work before being called away for the fire.

"I'll get you dropped off then."

"Cheers," I said, already opening my phone, which I'd stored in the glovebox, and shooting Ross a message to say thank you.

"It would be good to catch a break tomorrow." Craig's words were followed by a jaw-cracking yawn.

I followed suit, yawning loudly and wishing the same thing. "Right. We need this weather to break, that's for sure. This whole hell-on-earth thing the country's emulating is the pits."

"I hear ya. Your boss still being good about you volunteering?"

I nodded, another yawn joining the action. "Yeah, Jacko's cool. His brother's a firie too, so he gets it." It would have been piss poor if he hadn't, especially in our relatively small county and with the high threat of continued fires still in our future.

"Your dad get home okay earlier?" I asked. Craig's dad, Tom, was a firie too and had been out early this morning.

"Yeah. He's fine. Got home and is resting up. He's keeping an eye on what's happening in Bulla Creek."

I frowned, all too aware that Bulla Creek was

seeing more action than us and that Craig's parents' place was one of the first larger properties that side of town.

"Just make sure you call if the threat is one we need to make note of, yeah?"

"Thanks, Dan." Craig cast me a small smile, his focus returning quickly to the darkening road ahead.

Craig's folks' place was like my second home, or maybe third, considering how I struggled to keep away from Ross's, despite the broken promise to do just that. The thought of his parents losing their place, and more importantly being in danger, sent a shot of unease in my gut.

We needed the weather to change. I didn't want this to become the norm—living in a constant state of dread.

But like everything, we'd ride it through and take the good with the bad. And knowing I had Ross making me lasagne and taking care of me from a distance was the reminder I needed that moving home was a good thing.

Before long, we were pulling up in front of my rental, and I was dragging my arse to the front door, having said goodbye to Craig. Once inside, I tugged off my boots and headed straight for the small laundry, where I stripped and shoved my clothes in the washing machine.

I pulled on a pair of shorts from the clean linen basket and immediately headed outside to the small beer fridge I kept out there next to my outdoor setting.

The smile on my face was immediate when I pulled out the container Ross had left me. On top was a sticky note.

Shower, eat, rest, and be safe!

I peeled the note off, and like the lovesick fool I was, stuck it to my fridge once in the kitchen. Placing the container in the microwave, I set the timer and then went to shower off. Ross's instructions were a no-brainer.

Dirty water soon swirled down the drain as I scrubbed at my skin, wrinkling my nose at the smell of smoke that clung to every pore on my body. Even after washing my hair twice, the scent remained, but the citrus helped wash some of it away. Though smelling like burnt orange wasn't perhaps the best scent ever.

It would have to do.

Throwing a clean pair of boxers on, I looked around my room, groaning at the pile of dirty laundry I'd yet to shift. For at least another day it would have to wait.

Honestly, I was just grateful for clean skin, carb-loaded food, and a bed to sleep in.

The air conditioning came a close fourth, and I switched on the unit in my bedroom to cool down my room. It wouldn't be long before I hit the hay, and a room that didn't resemble an oven would mean I'd settle better.

After juggling the hot container with my food, I carried the plate to the sitting room and picked up my phone.

A quick call to Ross would make sleep come swifter. Knowing he was okay and simply hearing his voice had become our nightly routine, unless I didn't get home till way past civilised o'clock. On those nights, I flicked Ross a text. Communication he asked for and contact I was more than happy to make.

It wasn't long past nine, so I hit his number on my phone. Two rings later, he answered, "Hey, everything okay?"

"Yeah. Managed to squash it. Everyone's safe. Knackered."

A soft exhale travelled down the line. My heart flipped at the sound. "Thank Christ. More and more reports are coming on the news about fires breaking out, some way out of control."

Tilting back my head, I sighed, tired and scared. "It's a shitshow."

"You sure you're okay?" Concern softened his voice, and I could imagine the tilt of his head, the tightness of his brows as he spoke.

"Yeah," I said, not quite sure if I was, not with so much happening in Australia. "I just need rest."

"You go eat. Actually, did you get your food?"

"Yeah," I answered with a smile, hoping he could hear my appreciation. "Thank you. Just about to eat it now. That doesn't mean you have to go." Ross's voice was soothing, a comfort I could happily embrace every day.

A yawn tore free, though, making him chuckle.

"And that's my cue. Don't forget to let me know you're safe tomorrow, okay?"

"Absolutely." Whether he expected the same from his brother and dad or not, I didn't know. All I knew was that he cared about me and wanted to make sure I got home safely every evening.

That knowledge was enough to ease some of the stress of the day.

"Night, Ross."

"Night, Dan."

We ended the call, and I went back to finishing the food he'd made me.

Once all of this craziness had calmed, perhaps it was time to let Ross know it was his quiet, steady reassurance that made me feel like I was home.

7

———

ROSS

It could be mistaken for fog, the visibility so low I was sure if I reached out, my hand would disappear. The acrid scent of burnt trees was the dead giveaway, though. It was too close for comfort. Too real.

Once more, I checked the Facebook page, scrolling through for updates. There was no mention of an immediate threat. No discussion of a fire within twenty kilometres or so, but this wasn't my first rodeo.

I'd seen first-hand how a stray spark could dance in the breeze and find purchase on dry leaves fifty metres away, lighting up the baked earth and the parched trees as quickly as a match.

Next, I checked my messages—Facebook and

general text—but there was nothing. Craig was out, called in from work again yesterday to suit up and head out to a small fire on the other side of town. My brother knew what he was doing. He'd been a rural firefighter since he was sixteen. Before that he'd hung out with Dad and Uncle Bill at the station from the time he was twelve, desperate for the chance to join up.

It didn't mean I worried less. Then there was this smoke. I knew rationally, it would have been the smoke from whatever fire my brother was helping to fight, probably twenty-five minutes or so drive away, but still, anxiety gnawed in my gut.

Devastation and loss were thick in the air from so many parts of the country. With the news of the destructive fires and their horrors trickling in fast and thick, I jumped between annoyance at myself for overthinking the dangers to our own region and desperation that I could be—*should be* doing something more.

For now, though, an update was all I needed. A simple okay would put me at ease, but instead, with smoke thick in the air, nothing could distract me. It didn't help that Dan was out as well.

I sighed and cracked my neck from side to side, attempting to release the build-up of tension settling there. The last thing I needed to think about was Dan. In doing so, my concern spiked further.

It had only been over the past three weeks or so that everything had finally settled between the two of us. While Dan's initial distance had hurt, I'd given him the space he needed, determined not to put pressure on the guy. But finally, after I'd figured out what the real problem was, I'd worked hard at making things right and getting back where we were—hanging out, having fun, and me struggling with being so hung up on him I couldn't see past him to date anyone else.

"Bloody hell," I grumbled, turning my back on the open valley and heading to my shed. I needed to stay active before I pulled my hair out or decided to do something reckless like jump in my Hilux and find the pair of them.

My brother and Dan weren't always known for thinking things through. Yeah, they were great at what they did, both in their day jobs and as rural firefighters, but that sometimes meant they went above and beyond. Running on lack of sleep and working overtime to catch up with days missed last week from tackling two localised bushfires meant they probably wouldn't be at their sharpest.

I exhaled loudly and started up my old Macy.

One of the paddocks had too much regrowth, especially considering the current dangers, so clearing it up was practical, and I hoped it would offer me the distraction needed.

Dust followed my path, the scorched earth offering nothing but a greater hazard to my visibility. I was certain the sun was pissed off, not being able to spread its searing heat through the smoke blanketing the earth. And while the respite from the sun's rays would have been welcome any other time, today, seeing clear blue skies and the relentless sun would have been a relief.

The vibration from my phone caught my attention. I braked, putting the old girl in neutral as I tugged my mobile out of my pocket. It was Mum.

"All okay?" I said on answer.

"I've heard from Dad." She sounded breathless, the slightest hint that something wasn't quite right not so well hidden in her shaky voice.

"Dad okay?"

"Yes," she rushed out, immediately making my heart stutter and try to beat more regularly. "He's helping coordinate things."

"Okay," I said slowly, waiting for her to get to the point of calling. I wasn't impatient by nature, but hell if these recent sparks didn't get me angsty. We were so lucky, incredibly so. In New South Wales and now Victoria, the flames were out of control. It was more like they were *in* control, destroying everything in their path and leaving nothing but devastation behind. So we were lucky in comparison. While fires continued to break out in our region, so far, our local rural firies were able to contain each and every one before they got out of hand.

The thought of them not being able to do so wasn't something I wanted to consider.

"He contacted me saying there's been a forecast for strong winds." I looked around me as she spoke, taking note of the gentle breeze brushing past the gum leaves and making the silky oaks rustle. "He's worried it'll push the fires further west."

"Towards you?" I said slowly, trying to keep my panic at bay. Mum and Dad lived about forty minutes northwest of me.

"I'm sure it'll be fine. You know what these weather reports are like." Her voice was tightly controlled. In my thirty-three years, I'd heard it several times, and usually when she was about to lose her shit at me, my brother, or Dad, or because she was afraid. With Craig and Dad being out all night, I imagined it was a combination.

"I'll head your way now."

"No, no." I could visualise her shaking her head, worrying her necklace as she spoke.

"Mum, I'm coming. Start sorting the horses. Get the float ready. I'll be there as quickly as I can."

"You sure?" And there was the relief. It was clear as day, despite her fear of being a bother.

"Of course I'm sure. Just keep your phone on you and keep your two-way open on the ATV if you use it. I'll be able to pick up a signal a few K out, just in case. Love you, Ma. See you soon."

"Thanks, Ross. Love you too. Drive safe."

I ended the call and immediately put the tractor in gear, my head already buzzing with what I needed to do.

While I knew they were fire prepared, fire wouldn't be bargained with or sweet-talked into being stamped out.

I packed up quickly before hightailing it out of my place and travelling towards my folks' property. About fifteen minutes in, my phone rang. I clicked my wheel, opened up the Bluetooth app, and registered my brother's name on the console.

"Craig," I greeted. "All good?"

"Yeah. You on the way to Mum?"

"About twenty minutes out," I said when I took in my surroundings. While I was driving carefully, the roads were clear, and I was hovering a fair bit above the speed limit.

"Good." I heard a noise in the background—the sound of an engine and voices and the distinct rumble of Dan's voice that had my heart hammering harder. "We're done here. Dan and I will meet you there. Dad shouldn't be far behind us."

My gut tightened, fear making my heart stutter. "So the threat's serious?" It seemed crazy asking that aloud, especially with so much destruction further south, with land, homes, and lives being taken, and while small bushfires weren't that uncommon, we'd never been under real threat before.

The closest I'd come was when I stayed at my aunt's down south when I was a teenager. The memory had left its mark.

"Seems that way. Hopefully the wind will calm so the Bulla Creek division can get on top of it their end, but we wanted to come just in case."

"And Dan?" I rolled my eyes, knowing he'd already told me Dan would be coming by to help, but honestly, I had no excuse other than my head was buzzing with information and dread made it difficult to process.

I didn't think I was cut out for this level of disaster.

I was a school librarian, for Christ's sake. It was the summer holiday, and that was the reason why I'd been able to keep on top of my small ten acres. The rest of the time, I let my cows and my two goats, Bessie and Benji, do the work.

I could wrangle three school classes in the tight confines of the library, no worries. I could even spot a shifty student trying to sneak their phone out of their bag, but this level of threat, it was the real deal. But now was not the time for freaking out. There was no time for that.

"Dan's safe and coming with," he answered, amusement in his voice. The arse knew I'd been crushing on his best mate since the time I discovered internet porn, even though I'd never said a thing and we'd never actually discussed it.

"I can make sure he's prepared for you to check him over thoroughly when we get there if you don't believe he's okay," he joked, surprising me. It had been a while since he'd teased me about Dan. "Remind him you've got farm-roughened hands despite all the hours you spend with books." His laughter was loud, making me smile and easing some of my panic. If he was laughing, it couldn't be as bad as I feared, surely. "I'm sure he'd appreciate a neck rub."

"Piss off." I shook my head, allowing a slight grin. I followed with "See you soon," just as I heard Dan ask, "Ross knows how to massage?"

I quickly hit the Cancel button on my wheel in horror. There was no doubt I would have closed my eyes and perhaps slammed my head against the wheel a few times if I wouldn't likely crash in the process. Once this was over, and my parents and their place were safe, I was kicking Craig's arse.

Plus, massage?

Okay, that thought had merits.

While my fingers would ache in probably five minutes, they'd be five minutes well spent if I could get my hands on Dan's naked skin.

8
———

DAN

THIS ONE HADN'T BEEN TOO BAD IN THE GRAND scheme of what was happening around our scorched country. I'd spent fifteen hours since last night helping to tackle this smaller blaze. The whole time, visibility had been barely three metres, and sweat had blurred my vision. Now, covered in soot, my protective gear sodden with sweat and charred bush-land—which I'd since stripped off and thrown on some clean clothes—I was ready for a hot shower and bed, even though it was only early afternoon.

But there was no chance of that.

The fire in our neighbouring region had caused a stir, and there was increasing chatter of it spreading. Any other time, I'd be racing over to lend a hand. With the state on high alert, crews were heading out to wherever they were needed, some setting off for days at a time.

It was only Craig's concern that had stopped me. I would have gone with him anyway to help his parents. They were the best of people, but when he'd said Ross was ahead of us and would be reaching his mum first, my heart had plummeted.

The thought of him facing a fire was enough to have me ignoring the layers of sweat and the exhaustion threatening the edges of my vision.

Adrenalin was a heady thing, and right now, I needed it to keep me vigilant and make sure the Fosters were okay, especially Ross.

"You all right over there?"

Craig's question made me jump. So focussed on staring out at the passing bush and thoughts on my friend's younger brother, it didn't seem I was up for any additional multitasking.

It was a good job he'd offered to drive. I'd been the one to collect him midway through work today, so we were in my Hilux, but I figured his offer was more about him focusing on something else and trying not to worry too much about his parents.

He chuckled a little. "Be sure to grab yourself a Hydralyte. Get that head of yours clear."

I grunted in response and reached over to the

back seat and swiped the small cooler bag. Two drinks in hand, I opened the lid of one and passed it to Craig before opening my own and taking a deep gulp.

I grimaced at the taste, but Craig was right. I needed to stay hydrated to remain alert.

"So, all okay?" he asked again after placing his bottle in the cupholder.

"Just tired." A jaw-cracking yawn followed, and I shook my head, trying to wake myself up. "You?"

He bobbed his head. "Will be. Just need to make sure Mum's safe, try to secure their property as much as possible, then hope like hell the wind drops and this brewing fire pisses off and dies."

"You and me both." I paused before saying, "And Ross?"

"Hmm?" The arsehole's lips twitched, and he didn't exactly try to hide his reaction to my question.

"Shut it. Your brother, how far ahead is he? He knows what he's doing, right?" Him not knowing didn't sit comfortably. Obviously, Ross wasn't a firie, but with his dad and brother active, he would have picked up enough, right?

Shit, we'd spent enough time together over the past few months, I should have checked.

The thought of his large brown eyes wide and

panicked had me shifting uncomfortably and darting my attention to the speedometer. A few kilometres over the limit, and I couldn't ask for more, no matter how much I wanted to.

"Not much more than us." Craig indicated right, slowing briefly before pulling into the road and once more accelerating. "He'll be fine. He knows how to prepare." A snort broke free from Craig as he continued, "Seriously, we had monthly fire drills at home for at least two years. Eventually Mum was able to talk Dad down to twice a year."

I grinned, relaxing a little. I'd forgotten Tom had done just that. I'd even been involved in a few of them.

"So did you go on that date Alec tried to set up for you?"

Frowning at the topic change, I glanced in his direction. "Nah. Didn't feel like it." The date he was talking about was meant to happen a couple of weeks ago, so Craig asking now was odd.

"No?"

I shook my head, and he knew exactly the reason why.

While I wanted the unspoken to happen, I was still a coward thinking about the what-ifs.

"Huh." He indicated once more to turn right. I

sat up a little, recognising we were only five minutes out from his parents' place.

His "huh" registered. A quick glance his way told me he was anxious. Understandable, considering the situation. Giving him a boon and providing him with a distraction, I bit. "Huh, what?"

A twitch of his lips followed. Yeah, I totally took the bait.

"Alec tried to set Ross up too."

Again? I wondered if it was with the same guy as before, but recalled Ross mention that had been with a guy he knew from the pub. I tensed a little at this new information. Alec was a good friend to all three of us. The "tried" in Craig's comment then clicked into place, finally working its way into my tired brain, and my shoulders relaxed a little.

I considered not questioning him, while wondering why he was talking about this now, considering the past couple of months we hadn't mentioned our conversation about Ross. Three minutes out and with the whitening of Craig's fingers on the steering wheel, I figured it would be worth it to help keep his anxiety at bay, knowing his focus was really on his parents. "'Tried' as in it didn't work out or Ross said no?" Admittedly I was curious and hoping for the latter. I also wondered why, once again, I hadn't known, but truth be told, I hadn't exactly advertised Alec trying to set me up either.

Craig's grin was quick to form. "Said no. Something about being busy, not being interested in meeting anyone *new*." The emphasis didn't go unnoticed. "Alec figures he's got a hard-on for someone we know."

I clamped my mouth shut, not willing to go there and trusting that Craig hadn't discussed my feelings for his brother with anyone else. Instead, I looked ahead and exhaled in relief when I saw the gates to his parents' property, and that while smoke hung low in the area, there was no intensity at the moment.

I eased myself higher in the passenger seat as we pulled into the long drive, both of us glancing around for signs of an immediate threat. As we pulled up close to the house, Harriet stepped out and waved. I threw my hand up in response, giving Craig's mum a small smile before scanning the area.

And there he was, leading his folks' two horses out of the stables. He paused, eyes landing on us. His relief was immediate—the smile, the relaxing of his shoulders, the movement of his lips that followed, suggesting he exhaled deeply.

My gaze didn't stray from him as I exited the car and stepped in his direction. Making sure he was coping was my priority.

9

———

ROSS

Just fixing my eyes on Dan made me shudder in the best of ways. My reaction was swiftly followed by relief. He was okay. He was here. Movement to his left, and I spotted my brother. I quickly sent him a wry grin. Yeah, I was pretty damn relieved Craig was safe and here too.

"How you doing?" Dan's question pulled my attention back to him. Concern and relief registered on his features. I knew the look all too well, as it reflected my own every time—in the past three weeks especially—when he'd been called out battling fires, to then return home safely.

"Good." I nodded, raking my eyes over his exhausted form. While his clothes were clean, his skin was not. "You sure you're okay to be here?"

He rolled his eyes as he stepped into my space, his one hand lifting to stroke my mum's mare, Mable. "I'm hardly not going to be here, am I?"

My stomach flipped at that.

"Your dad would kick my arse if I let anything happen to his place, or more importantly, to your mum."

The tingly feeling in my gut dissipated. Dan was here for my folks, my family. I knew that. And while I was grateful, the moment I'd allowed myself to consider that I was his focus was a foolish pursuit. He wasn't interested, something I kept forgetting.

Instead, I shook my disappointment aside and allowed my gratitude that he was here for my parents to sink in and roll over me. He was such a good guy, regardless of his interest in me being nothing more than concern for a friend. I pulled a smile out and let it settle naturally on my face. "True," I finally answered, probably a beat too late. "My old man on the way?"

He nodded, then stepped to the side to take the horse's reins from me so I could focus on Charlie. "Hopefully he shouldn't be long. We were lucky that last blaze got under control so quick." He shook his head, and frustration and worry dipped his brows low.

"What's wrong?" I asked.

"My mate Davey was sent down to Mallacoota." He shook his head as my understanding registered. News about the small town has spread far and wide. Images of the blazing red sky had burned into my memory. *Dante's Inferno* seemed epitomised in the images I'd seen. I couldn't even begin to imagine the horror and fear the people of the town, and countless other people hit by the same burning wrath, experienced as the fires mercilessly wiped out their homes and took the lives of their loved ones.

I swallowed hard and reached out, my hand settling on Dan's forearm. I squeezed, hoping the small gesture would at least let him know he wasn't alone. I hated to ask, but I couldn't not. "Is he okay?"

When he nodded, relief whooshed through me. I moved my hand away only to pause, my heart accelerating hard when he reached out and clamped his hand around my forearm. My small smile disappeared as question filled my eyes. My heart didn't slow down its wild beat as his fingers slipped, never severing contact, until his hand shifted and his palm gripped mine.

It was his turn to squeeze and my turn to wonder what the hell was happening.

"Davey's fine. Thank God," he said, barely above

a whisper. "It was scary stuff, and a part of me wishes I was heading down there to support him and so many others who've flown in."

I blanched, my fingers constricting around his hand. As soon as I realised I gripped him, I attempted to ease away, but his firm hold prevented me.

"If I wasn't needed here, I probably would." His gaze remained on mine. His pupils danced, as if searching my own for something.

I managed to bob my head. "It must be hard staying back," I said. "But look where you were today. Look where we are now." While I hoped the preparation was a false alarm and came to nothing, the possibility it wouldn't be made it difficult to think straight. "I'm glad you're here." Dan had a calmness to him that sometimes was at odds with his jokester personality. But whenever he was nearby, he had a way of enabling me to relax, especially if I'd had a crap of a day at work.

"Me too." His voice remained low, his focus intent.

"You about done?" Craig's voice had me tearing my focus and my hand away.

I cleared my throat and nodded at my bemused-looking brother. "Just about." I wanted to wince at the weird pitch to my voice but held strong.

"Good." His attention shifted to Dan. "When you've finished, help me hitch up the water tanker."

"Will do," Dan answered, his voice completely unaffected.

"I can finish off here if you want?" I cast a quick glance Dan's way as I spoke.

He shook his head. "Let me help. We'll get it done quicker."

I agreed, knowing he was right. I'd already attached the trailer to Mum's vehicle, so it would mean I could head back in and see what else needed doing.

Between the two of us, we made quick work of settling the horses. In that time, the smoke had thickened, even denser than it was at my place. The wind had shifted slightly, not helping the smoke clawing its way around the property and surrounds. I just hoped it wasn't helping the fire along, and that the firies assigned to the burn were doing okay, keeping safe, and winning the fight.

"Stay safe, yeah?"

The closeness of Dan's voice took me by surprise. My drifting off worrying about the fire was dangerous if it meant I wasn't paying attention.

"Sure thing," I answered, hoping he hadn't seen my small jolt. I angled towards the man at my side, my heart stuttering once more, but this time in reaction to him flicking his attention briefly to my mouth.

I daren't hope that it was the universal sign for wanting a kiss. That could only lead to humiliation and heartbreak. Plus, this was so not the time. I seriously needed to get my head on straight.

"You stay safe too." I managed a grin before stepping away from him and bounding towards the house in search of Mum.

"That you, Ross?" Mum called out as soon as my boots thudded on the hallway floorboards.

"Yep. Where do you need me?"

Mum proceeded to set me to task. We were still planning to secure the property should the fire edge closer, but she wanted to prepare should they need to evacuate too.

Fifteen minutes into loading the car with some files, I headed outside to see if Craig needed help. As I made my way towards him and Dan while they secured hoses to Dad's water tanker, which was by far older than I was, my attention was diverted to the driveway and the oncoming vehicle.

Dad was home.

10

DAN

We'd laid out pipe, shifted the spare fuel from the shed, and I was just about to head up to double-check the guttering when I waved at Tom as he stepped out of his car. Exhaustion marred his features, yet he still held a smile before heading to the main water hose.

I carried on with my task, aware the smoke wasn't easing and the wind continued to build. While it was important to hope the crew working the fire a few kilometres away was not only safe but successful, the reality of needing to be prepared sat heavily on my chest.

After seeing the gutters were clear, I worked through my mental checklist, trying to ensure if the fire came this way, we could try to stop it in its tracks, and if we were unsuccessful, that we'd done enough to protect as much of the house as possible.

Too many Australians had already lost so much. I didn't want that to happen to the Fosters. The knowledge they were insured offered a semblance of relief, but that wouldn't help the heartbreak that came with losing the property they'd worked so hard for.

"Dan." Craig's call reached me, the urgency clear.

I descended the stepladder and jogged to the front of the house. He stood with his parents and Ross.

"Mum's going to head on out and take her car and the horses to Ross's," Craig explained.

It made sense. Even if the fire didn't catch up, it was best to be prepared, just in case. I nodded. "What's the plan? Any news?" After the barest of glances at Ross, my gaze travelled to Tom, who remained rigid, eerily so.

"I've just spoken to Mike. They seem more confident they've contained the area near the creek, but they're worried about the wind." Tom cast a concerned glance at his wife, no doubt aware that her worry would increase if he said much more. "Let's just get Harriet out on the road, and we'll see what else needs doing."

He led Harriet to the SUV by the hand, leaning close and speaking quietly. She bobbed her head a few times. Her fear, though, was palpable, walloping me in the gut. Harriet was like a second mum to me. I had very few memories growing up that didn't feature one of the Fosters. I glanced away when she pulled Ross into a hug, too tempted to suggest he go with her. There was no chance he'd go, though, not yet. Ross was a special breed of stubborn when he wanted to be, but there was no way I'd allow him to put himself at risk. If it came down to it, I'd throw him in the back of his ute and strap him down and race him out of here.

"Dan, get yourself over here." The emotion in Harriet's voice didn't sit right, flickering to life my own concern.

A small smile formed on my lips as I embraced her. She'd know it was fake.

"Don't you dare put yourself at risk." Her voice was low against my ear. "And you make sure you look after that boy of mine." She finished with a squeeze and pulled away. I simply bobbed my head, more than aware that she knew I would always look out for Ross. The woman was too damn perceptive.

As she pulled away a few moments later, Tom let the full extent of his fear be known. The lines around his eyes appeared more pronounced, the redness in his eyes reflecting the exhaustion beating at him. "It's likely that the wind will push the fire this way." He cast his focus in the direction of the large gum about twenty metres from his house; its leaves were swaying with increasing speed. The smoke tickled my nose already, threatening to make me sneeze, and while it wasn't that dense, the likelihood it would be soon was high.

"We continue to soak and try our hardest to ensure nothing comes close to the house," Tom said, his voice clear. "Craig, you focus on the water truck, and we'll use the embankment as our marker to call in for help if anyone is available; if not, we'll then use the midway pipeline as our point to leave, okay?"

Knowing that walking away would be so damn hard, I nodded, but our lives were so much more important. If we couldn't control the flames by the point he'd said, there was no way we'd be able to once the house's wooden frame caught—certainly not without the fire truck here.

"Ross, the embankment is your cue to leave and get to your pla—"

"Not a chance," he said, interrupting his dad. "I'll go when you go."

Tom's gaze hardened as he looked at Ross; mine did too, ready to back the old man up should I need to. "This is non-negotiable. You aren't trained like your brother and Dan."

Ross flicked his attention to me, steely determination set in eyes I'd missed over the years. I quirked my right brow in challenge, hoping he read my face clearly. He wouldn't be getting support from me. His eyes narrowed a little before he returned his attention to his dad. "I know enough to be helpful. I'm not going to be all gung-ho and put myself or anyone else at risk." He shook his head. "Give me some credit." He then focussed on his brother. "Craig, come on. Us even talking about this is ridiculous and wasting time."

I jerked my head in Craig's direction.

His eyes were on Tom. "Ross is right, Dad. We're wasting time. He's not stupid when it comes to shit like this." Craig's support was immediate.

"No." The loudness of my voice seemed to startle us all. But the word was out there now, and all eyes were on me.

A crease wrinkled Ross's forehead. "No?" He shook his head. "Seriously, it's not like you or anyone," he said pointedly, "has a say. Now get your heads out of your arses and—"

"I'm serious." I didn't flinch, didn't ease my focus away. Instead, my sight was locked on Ross and his heating cheeks. No doubt anger and frustration were the cause, but I didn't care what shit was thrown my way. I'd follow through with my promise to protect him.

"And why the hell—"

Once again, I cut him off. But this time, I would slice through all the BS and shut this down for good. A niggle in my mind told me I was being a domineering prick, but I could live with that if it meant Ross was safe. "I won't be able to keep you safe while trying to put out damn fires." My tone remained even despite the acceleration of my heart.

"Oh, hell," Craig said, followed by a snort. "Dad, come on. Let's carry on and let the caveman here do his thing."

Not flipping Craig the finger took restraint, and I could only imagine what his dad's reaction was—something I'd worry about later. My whole focus was on Ross and the widening of his eyes and the change in the set of his shoulders when my words seemed to hit their mark.

"What exactly are you saying?"

I grinned despite the panic edging its way into my chest that I was actually going to do this, loving how he stepped up to the challenge. Of course, now was so beyond not the right time to be airing my feelings for the guy. But sometimes opportunities came along in the most bizarre of moments. I'd be a fool to ignore this one and not seize the opportunity.

When Ross stepped into my space rather than me making the move, my heart flipped over. His brows rose in expectation, egging me on.

"My focus is always on you," I admitted. "You being so close to a situation you've not been trained for means I won't be able to do my job properly." I wanted to swallow, to clear my throat, but instead, I ploughed on. "I need you to let me help your dad and your brother. I need you to not feel as though you have to step beside any of us in this situation." My voice dipped, and my gaze slowly flicked to his eyes and then his mouth. "And I need for you to let me kiss you, just so I know I'm not imagining this."

It was out there—my words, my emotions, my truth. There was no taking them back. Relief spread into my veins, knowing I no longer had to keep wondering about the possibility of there being an us. It wasn't until he smiled and grasped my shoulder, though, that finally, despite the shitty situation, despite his stubborn arse, I knew somehow we'd get through all of this intact.

11

ROSS

THERE WASN'T TIME TO SAVOUR THE FEELING OF his lips against mine, nor was there time to commit his taste to memory. Even though fleeting, the kiss was searing, real, and everything I'd hoped it would be.

I pulled away first, his shoulder still in my grip, my lips searing from the connection. "Okay," I said breathlessly, the one word sounding distant beneath the loud pounding of my heart. I would help for as long as it was safe and then head to mine. Craig was right when he said I wasn't stupid, and honestly, my debating wasn't a pissing contest. It was all about me protecting my parents' home. End of story. "I'll leave when it's time, and then we'll talk about this later."

I glanced at his lips, tempted to press mine to

them again, but I was not a horny teenager with no self-control. There was also the fact that the smoke was irritating my eyes and standing outside was becoming increasingly uncomfortable.

But hell, that kiss.

I held back the shudder at the taste of him, despite how brief it was. Now was the time to focus.

The smile that lifted his lips was worth my acquiescence. I'd been on the receiving end of his smile many times over the years, but this smile was definitely different. I could get used to the softness in his gaze, the care so obviously directed my way.

"Thank you." He shifted his arm that had made its way around my waist and took hold of my hand. "I promise we'll talk about this later." The sound of gravel had us both looking towards the interruption. Craig watched on with a smug grin.

"Come on. Dad needs you." He rolled his eyes at, I assumed, the pair of us before heading back to the house.

"Not the best time for this, right?" I said.

Dan shrugged. "Maybe not, but I needed to say it."

My heart tripped over itself. "I'm glad." I pulled away, only hesitating a moment before I brushed my lips over his and stepped away fully. I couldn't not.

After battling my feelings, after reading this whole situation so wrong, I needed enough kisses to prove this was all real. "I'm heading to the house. Stay safe."

"Will do," he called after me, his voice gruff, as I focussed ahead rather than staring back at him. It wasn't the time for tripping and falling on my arse.

"What's next?" I said when I spotted Dad, my breathing as regular as I could make it.

The question in his stare was teamed with an amused smile. "So, you and Dan, huh." He shook his head, and I focussed on the smudge on his face, trying to stop myself from shifting uncomfortably. "Your mum totally called that one. Me, I wasn't so sure."

Surprise fluttered awake. While Dad and I had a decent relationship, we didn't really talk about my dating life.

With no idea how to respond, I settled on, "Um, okay?"

Smile still in place, Dad placed his hand on my shoulder. "We both know he's a good guy." I nodded, agreeing completely. "Now, let's finish off out here."

Ease settled into my limbs. It was the weirdest of days. Competing with the fear of the fire and the adrenalin pumping in my veins and making my head spin was the crazy new development with Dan. While I'd given up hoping it would happen at some point, it actually happening threatened to spin me out of control. It was not the time for that, especially as I helped Dad refuel the pumps to our dams to soak the ground.

Dripping with sweat and squinting into the distance just over an hour later, I swallowed hard. Light grey smoke no longer filled the valley. Instead, a cloying grey verging on black wafted up, rolling our way. My gaze shifted, following the plumes. There it was. The first flicker of orange.

We'd been expecting it. Dad had received a call not long ago, letting us know a team behind the fire headed our way. They were successfully dowsing the flames the crawling fire left in its wake, and while they were catching up with it, they'd come a little unstuck when they'd had to hang back to tackle the bushland.

Heat brushed my side, but this heat was welcome. "You okay?" Dan asked. Surprise had me glancing down when he took my hand in his, the move natural and as though he'd done it a hundred times before. His grasp was firm, comforting.

"Dad seems to think we've got this."

"You don't think we have?" Dan asked.

I shrugged, feeling a little guilty at my admission. "I trust him and know he has years of experience, but it's right there." I nudged my chin in the direction of the fire that already had inched closer. While it was still a fair distance away, the sight incited nothing but dread.

"The firies tackling it are doing a great job. If we keep watching the horizon, we'll see them following. But this is where our hard work comes in. Your dad's already spoken to his team; they're helping Bruce and Janie."

I nodded, relieved they were helping my parents' neighbours prepare.

"Once they've secured the property, they're going to start meeting the blaze from the south. We've got this." He squeezed my hand. "Can you head to the shed and soak the roof?"

My eyes met his at his request. Logically I knew it was preventative stuff, but my gut tightened at just how close the fire was and that quite possibly, it could reach the shed, then the house, then—

"Hey." Dan's firm grip on my forearms wrenched me out of my panic. This was the reason why I wasn't a firie. Pressure wasn't new to me, but what my dad, my brother, Dan, and every other firefighter had to handle was unsurmountable for me to truly comprehend. I had no idea how Dan appeared so calm by my side. There was no panic in his eyes, no anxiously dipped brow, no sweat pouring down his temple.

"You're incredible." The words spilled out of me as I searched his eyes. My attention flicked to his mouth, and his lips quirked.

"I think you're incredible too." While sounding deeper than usual, his voice was alight with tenderness and just a smidge of humour.

With a quick roll of my eyes and a nudge against him, I finally smiled back. "Thank you."

He nodded. I hoped it was in understanding that I was grateful for him helping me keep my sanity.

"I'll head to the shed now." I turned to leave, but he tugged at my arm. Question filled my focus as I looked back at him.

"Put the protective gear on before you start. It's by the tap."

"Whose is it?" My brow furrowed. I was all too aware of how little the rural firies got in terms of protective gear and equipment. To have a spare was never heard of. My eyes widened. "I'm not wearing your gear." I had no idea if it was even here, but I was already shaking my head. There was no way Dan could be left vulnerable.

"It's not mine." He gave a single shake of his head. "It's your dad's ancient one. Probably stinks." He winked at that and indicated for me to leave.

"Thanks for that, arsehole." I grinned, turned, and jogged in the direction of the shed, ready to get suited up and then carry on with my task.

12

DAN

The heat was intense but still bearable. Hope flickered to life in my chest. It appeared to be a surface fire, and with few trees and no bushland between Tom's place and the flames, the embers weren't spiralling out of control. The fire was low as it crawled across the grass, something similar to how a wave petered out and swept over the shore.

But there was no pulling back on this one. No tide to offer relief and keep it contained.

Instead, there was us and the sodden ground, which finally seemed to be slowing the spread a little. The closer it edged towards Tom's land, the less fuel it had to feed its flames.

"Is it me or is it slowing down?" Ross asked from a few metres away.

"It's not you," I called to him, not taking my eyes off the fire.

"That's good, right?" His voice was closer, and I risked a look, my lips twitching at the ancient protective gear he wore.

I refocussed on the flames and tilted my head when I heard one of the pumps cut out.

"I'll get it," Ross said immediately, racing off before I even had a chance to respond. That was fine by me. The diesel and the dam were in the opposite direction of the fire.

"The wind's calmed," Craig said as he stepped beside me. He'd just finished moving some of the pipe to drench a different part of the paddock. The wetter and cooler the ground, the better.

"Yeah." I nodded. While hope was alive, my adrenalin remained as anxiety gnawed at my gut. We'd all been working our arses off to prepare and prevent. Tiredness threatened the edges of my vision. A crash and burn was in my future, and I'd be grateful for it. It meant this time we'd won. We just weren't quite there yet.

With the bushfire seemingly now contained and our focus on the grassfire, visibility was a little clearer. Smoke remained heavy but not quite as dark.

"Here."

A drink appeared before me, and I gratefully took it from Craig. "Thanks." I unscrewed the top and gulped down the water.

"I'm going to fill the water truck back up, just in case," Craig explained. The truck was by far the most incredible vehicle Tom had. It meant we'd been able to head further than the pipes could reach and was one of the reasons why the fire was calming.

I nodded. "Stay safe." I waved him off and continued shifting the pipework from the opposite side of the paddock Craig had been working.

It was easier without the flow of water, and honestly, with the way everything was going, this section would get some seriously healthy grass soon enough, as the fire seemed to be holding off.

With a refill of the truck, Craig and Tom should be able to secure the property completely and smother the last of the grassfire.

I heaved up the pipe and turned to hold it behind me so I could drag it to where I wanted it. The weight was a struggle, especially with my shaky limbs from too much exertion and not enough sleep. With a grunt, I hauled it with me, continuing walking as far as the pipe would let me and to where I spotted the first piece of dry grass. Breathing heavily, I sucked in a deep breath, trying to regulate myself. I winced and coughed, ready to roll my eyes at myself for the action.

I could really have done with my breathing apparatus, but that had gone back to the station to be restocked when I'd left the crew a few hours earlier.

Pipework in place, it was ready to go. I stilled, realizing the sound of the closest pump should have been going by now. It wasn't that far away. Unease that Ross had stumbled across a problem hit me hard. With nothing to do here but wait for water and worry about Ross, I hightailed it towards the dam. I expected he would have grabbed the ATV to haul the diesel to the pump, which meant I'd have to go by foot.

As I passed by the shed, I registered the ATV was gone. I jogged in the direction of the dam, where I'd hoped to hear the sound of a growling diesel engine. No sound travelled towards me. I focussed on the direction of where the dam was, looking for a glimpse of Ross. There was no sign of the ATV or Ross. Before long, I reached the dam wall, out of breath and my nerves rattled.

Where the hell was he?

A quick scan around me held no answers.

Knowing he wouldn't have headed elsewhere without a legit reason, I considered my options. There would have been no reason to move beyond this dam. Nothing more than pastureland lay in that direction. Turning back towards the fire as I stood on the dam wall, I scanned to the right. Beyond the house, a flash of movement had me pausing and focussing hard. I held my breath for one beat, then two, before I finally exhaled once a shape formed.

With no idea why he'd ventured away from his task, I could do nothing but head towards him. He hadn't left the fuel here, hadn't been here from the lack of fresh tyre tracks. While the initial urgency of the grassfire wasn't completely over, we were no longer on high alert. But still, the pump still needed to be started.

Wishing like hell I didn't have to run made no difference. There was nothing but my tired feet that would get me to him. I didn't like that he was closer to where the dwindling fire was in the distance. Nor did I like that smoke obscured my view of him.

I pumped my arms faster, wanting to get to him quickly, check he was safe, and then get the final soaking of the ground sorted.

Maybe I could then finally head home, ideally

after a goodbye kiss from the pain in my arse known as Ross, and with a confirmed date for tomorrow.

Within shouting distance at last, I hollered, "Ross, what are you doing?" I could just make out his messy hair. He also no longer wore his protective jacket.

He angled his head towards me, his eyes wide. A wince followed by a grimace lit his face along with him mouthing, "Sorry."

Close enough now to read his mouthed words, I frowned, my eyes travelling his form. Something was amiss. It was then he turned. His arms were full, heaped with his protective coat, which appeared to be covering something.

"Shh," he hushed, jiggling the lump in his arms. "It's fine. I've got you."

Finally before him, I huffed out heavy breaths. "What's going on?" I nodded towards the moving form in his arms.

"I just happened to spot her when I wasn't far from the shed." He shifted a little, repositioning what I assumed was a creature of some sort, before reaching out and shifting the side of the coat. "She still has her baby with her. We need to get them to the vet."

I peered into the coat, my eyes widening at the soot-coated grey fur. "A koala?"

Ross bobbed his head as we fell in step towards the ATV a few metres away. "Yeah. She has a baby clinging to her but didn't give me much of a fight when I managed to swoop the pair of them up." He climbed in, and I settled behind the wheel. "Shit, the pump. I'm so sorry."

Relief that he was okay eased into me. A smile formed on my face. He was okay. "No worries. You did the right thing. Everything's in control."

Ross exhaled, his own smile lifting his lips. "Thank you. You can fill it up while I make some calls to find out the best place to take her to be looked at. Can you grab my phone out of my pocket?"

I side-eyed him, giving him a small grin. It didn't matter that I was shattered, that we'd been battling fire, that he was snuggled up with a koala. There was always time for my thoughts to go *there*.

He rolled his eyes and snorted before looking at his bundle and clamping his mouth shut.

I started the engine and drove to the dam. "Was she injured?" I asked, wisely changing the subject from the one about me putting my hand in his pants —pocket... whatever.

"I think so. Not badly, or at least I don't think. She was sort of hobbling, so maybe burnt paws."

"Most likely. Your brother managed to rescue a possum yesterday."

"The thought of how much we've lost is terrifying." His voice dipped, and sadness filled it. I got it. We—us, Australia, the land—had lost so much. It would be a while before we knew the real cost or the ramifications of so much loss. I could only hope that we, as a people, a country, did what we did best and rallied.

"I know. We just need to keep doing our part," I said as I parked.

After pulling out his phone and patting myself on the back for only offering a small wink in the process, I filled up the pump while I heard Ross speaking on the phone. All set, I headed back to the shed, waiting to hear what Ross said and determined to finish this final soak.

The sound of a familiar engine had me looking at the drive. A smile quickly formed, and I waved, spotting Frank behind the wheel.

The cavalry was here.

I switched off the engine and peered at Ross, who smiled and indicated I should head on out as he continued his call. I did so, but not until I leaned over and dotted a kiss on his mouth. His eyes widened a fraction before they softened. Following up with a wink, I headed over to Frank and the crew, who were stepping out of the fire truck.

"Frank," I greeted, reaching out and shaking his hand. "Good to see ya."

"You too, though I'm sure you wished your shift had been over, right?"

I snorted at that. "No such shifts, really, this season."

"True that," he answered before nodding to my right and greeting Tom.

After a few exchanges and the words "fully in control" and "no fresh spread," I exhaled loudly. Weight eased and fell away from my shoulders while my adrenalin waned.

"You doing all right there, Dan?"

Frank's voice pulled me out of my stupor. "Huh?" I glanced at him, not realising I'd zoned out so completely. My limbs felt heavy, and my brain struggled to catch up.

"Right, new plan," Frank said. He glanced over my shoulder, and I followed his line of sight, startled to see Ross standing just a little behind me. Concern marred his features. "Ross, take Dan with you before he falls on his arse and we have to scrape him up. Go do what you have to do with the koalas you found, then take him home and make sure he doesn't drown in the shower or something."

"Hey," I finally managed, my brain trying to catch up. "I'm good to finish off with the—"

"Benny is already on it." Frank quirked his brow at me in challenge, and I looked over and realised Benny did, in fact, have it.

"No worries. I've got Craig too and will drop him off on the way to the vet's. It's on the way. I'll take my truck, and we can sort out Dan's tomorrow." Ross reached out and placed his hand on my forearm, giving a small tug.

I considered saying something else. Being rail-roaded was not how things usually played out for me, but hell, I was bone-weary.

"Thanks, son." Tom bobbed his head at Ross before flicking his own concerned stare at me. Shit, how did he not look as wrecked as me? "Go. You've done back-to-back call-outs, worked at least double what I've done." The man was a goddamn mind reader. But I supposed he knew me far too well.

"'Kay," I settled on. "Thanks, but call if anything changes or you need me?"

"Sure thing," Tom answered, amused.

Yeah, I wasn't quite sure I believed him.

"Come on, let's get these koalas where they need to go, and you home." Ross's hand took mine, and I allowed myself the moment to savour the contact and the newness of it all. I seriously was tired, so much so, I was becoming increasingly worried about what I may say in my exhausted state.

He led me to his vehicle and edged me towards the passenger seat.

"I've got it." I grinned at him when he tried to buckle me in. "It's sweet though," I said, causing him to grin and lean in and place a kiss on my waiting mouth.

"Seriously, I can't be dealing with your level of loved up." Craig's loud groan followed. "Definitely not in such close proximity." He yawned. "And I swear," he said around a second yawn, "if I dream about the two of you doing that, I'll kick both your arses." His shudder was dramatic and almost warranted me reaching into the back seat and punching him in the arm. I didn't have the energy to follow through.

"Frank said Ross needed to make sure I wouldn't drown in the shower," I said instead, just as the man of my shower fantasies opened the door and sat behind the wheel. "Just some extra fodder for your nightmares, Craig."

Ross snorted and shook his head. I grinned. Poor Craig moaned to the point I was concerned I'd pushed him over the edge. But honestly, he'd pushed for this... or at least pushed for me to pull my head out of my arse.

It was official. My head was well and truly out and all up in Ross's business.

"I'm going to ignore everything you just said and put my whole energy into soothing this cute koala and her baby and hoping like hell positive karma comes my way and erases everything that came before."

I laughed and reached over the console and took Ross's hand in mine, giving it a light squeeze. "I can probably handle a shower by myself," I reluctantly admitted in a whisper.

Ross put the car in Drive and pulled away, his attention flicking my way. A smile turned up his lips. "I'm not quite sure you've seen the level of soot and dirt on you." He squeezed my hand back. "Those hard-to-reach places are going to need a definite helping hand."

Heat unfurled in my gut. I liked the sound of that a hell of a lot.

After a few moments and Ross yawning like it was going out of fashion, I demanded he pulled over so I could drive. He grumbled, ridiculously so, complaining that I needed to rest more than him considering I'd been awake for so long, and while I was shattered, the man was dead on his feet. I expected the adrenalin crash from worrying about his parents was hitting him hard.

We were quiet the rest of the drive, all of us exhausted from the madness of the day. Craig had fallen asleep about two minutes after I'd swapped seats with Ross, and Ross's eyes had slid shut about five minutes after.

The past few weeks had been full-on, the past thirty-six hours or so more so than usual. I flicked my gaze at Ross. His chest lifted and relaxed, his breathing quiet in comparison to his brother's.

I'd spent many nights sharing the same space as Ross—and his brother—when camping and such, but tonight would be phenomenally different.

Well, likely tomorrow morning, considering after a shower—where in truth I expected to prop Ross up rather than the other way around—Ross needed to simply sleep, as did I. But my plan was to be wrapped around him, and from the crackling heat between us earlier, I was confident he was on board.

I'd waited so long for this, danced around it to

the point of frustration. In truth, I'd half given up on the possibility.

When I'd reached for him just a few short hours ago, something had snapped inside me. The reality of the danger we were in, the folly of not pursuing something with Ross finally clicked into place.

And my mouth on his, Ross reciprocating... it all made sense and was absolutely worth the risk.

I pulled up outside of the vet where the wildlife contact had said he'd meet us. I climbed out, not waking up either of the sleeping men, then headed to the closed door. I rapped my knuckles against the wooden door. A few beats later, I heard movement, so stepped back a little.

An older guy in his midfifties answered, a warm smile on his face. "Ross?" he asked.

I reached out and shook his offered hand. "Dan. Ross is getting some shut-eye."

Understanding registered in his stare. "It's not pretty out there, is it?" I shook my head. "I'm Harry. Thanks so much for the rescue. What shape are they in?"

I led him to the car, saying, "The mum was walking, somewhat tentatively from what Ross said. The baby was wriggling around a fair bit. They're dirty, so I wasn't sure about burns or anything." I made to pull open the car door, only to jerk back when Craig beat me to it.

"Hey," he said with a yawn. "I've got her."

The driver door then opened, and bleary-eyed, Ross stumbled out as well. "Hey," he greeted, his gaze immediately snagging my own. "All okay?"

I smiled softly at him. "Yeah, all good. Just handing the koalas over to Harry here."

Harry nodded his greeting and took the box off Craig. "You all look like you've had a hell of a day."

Craig grunted. "Few weeks more like."

Sorrow etched over Harry's face. "It's all so devastating. Just when we think we're in the clear, something else sparks up." He offered a tentative smile to us all. "Thanks so much for being out there and battling."

Ross moved to stand by my side, his arm brushing mine. The invisible thread between us pulled and I leaned into him. "And thank you for all the work you're doing with these guys too," Ross said, indicating towards the box. "We all have to do our bit."

Harry's smile was wide, his eyes tired. I expected he was as shattered as we all were. "There's a storm coming in though, expected this Tuesday."

God, what we wouldn't do for rain. Heavy downpours of the good stuff to saturate the land and stimulate life and growth. "Let's hope so," I said.

"You guys be off and get yourselves cleaned up and to bed. Looks like you need to switch off for a while. Are you on call tomorrow?" he asked.

Craig rubbed a weary hand over his face. "Everyone is pretty much on call 24/7 at the moment."

I grimaced at that, selfishly hoping the fires would be kind and calm down, allowing us the rest we needed.

Ross turned and looked at me. "You're not at work tomorrow, are you?"

It was the last thing I needed, but I was all too aware bills didn't pay themselves. "Yeah, but not till midday. Jacko already texted to let me know a late start and half a shift was fine."

It was a relief I could at least sleep in.

"I'm heading into work to continue doing the community stuff."

I nodded at Ross as he spoke. Over the past couple of weeks, he'd been doing a few shifts at the school, opening the library doors to support families with kids during this crazy time.

We said goodbye to Harry and climbed back into the car. First stop was Craig's.

"You going to be okay?" I asked through the open window after he exited.

He bobbed his head heavily up and down, exhaustion evident in his stare. "Yeah. Nothing that a shower and sleep won't fix." Just as he turned to leave, he angled back towards us, leaning in. "Neither of you screw this up, yeah?"

My eyes sprang open. While my friend seemed okay with his brother and me finally admitting our attraction for each other, I understood his concern, since it had been hanging over our heads for seemingly forever. Glancing at Ross, I wondered what he was thinking, how he'd react. His attention was already directed my way.

A serious expression marred his tired face. After a moment of his eyes raking over me, he reached out and took my hand. "We won't screw this up."

That he was talking to me rather than his brother sent my heart bouncing around in my chest. Sincerity and warmth threaded every word, every breath, every touch.

Craig tapped the car roof, muttering, "Best bloody not," before walking away. The sound of his heavy footsteps the only thing letting me know he'd headed away since my eyes remained connected to Ross's.

"Ready?" he asked.

I quickly nodded, reluctantly releasing his hand as I returned my palms to the wheel. "Definitely," I whispered, pulling away and directing the car to my place.

13

—————

ROSS

It was a sorry state of things when I had the first opportunity to get up close and personal with a naked Dan, and I was too buggered to do anything about it. We'd considered not showering together, worried about wandering hands when one, we were both knackered and two, we both wanted to be fully alert to appreciate the moment.

But thank Christ we'd agreed we could handle the temptation. If it wasn't for Dan scrubbing me down with a soapy washcloth, I would have simply ended up on the shower floor, asleep, still dirty, and quite possibly at risk of drowning.

I felt guilty as hell that he was the one caring for me after he'd done so many hours and battled so many flames. But today had taken it out of me.

Adrenalin crashes were shit, reinforcing I wasn't made for this high-octane drama and responsibility.

"Come on." Dan's voice was gentle as he held my hand and led me out of the shower.

I was vaguely aware of him rubbing me down with a towel and thought I mumbled, "Thanks," before he steered me to his bedroom and indicated I should get under the covers. I didn't have time to savour the knowledge I was in his bedroom. I was simply impressed I was aware enough to know he'd brought me to his home—a place I'd visited regularly recently, usually leaving food in the beer fridge he kept out back.

As soon as my head connected with the soft cushion, I was already being dragged towards sleep, and when the heat of Dan's body wrapped around me from behind, I drifted into oblivion.

When I awoke the next morning to the warmth of Dan, I couldn't remember being more comfortable. We'd moved around in the night. One of my arms was wedged under his pillow, and Dan's cheek was pressed against my chest, his leg against mine. Never being a cuddler, the ease of the closeness bewildered me. But this was Dan, who I'd known forever. Not only that, but it had been a long time since my thoughts about him stepped way out of the bounds of friendship.

Awareness of his hand sweeping across my stomach had me angling and looking his way. He tilted his head, eyes groggy, but his smile was immediate and made my heart flip over.

"Morning." Gravelly with sleep, his voice was what I knew future fantasies were made of.

"Morning."

He angled even more, and I took my cue, happily pressing my lips to his. His soft lips were gentle, feeling right pressed against mine.

"You sleep okay?" he asked, releasing a yawn.

"Like a log." While this wasn't unusual for me, as I could sleep pretty much anywhere, having Dan flush against me made it the best way to ever wake up.

"Any idea what time it is?" Gentle fingers brushed across my stomach hairs.

"No idea. And I have no idea where my phone is." He'd taken care of me last night. No man had ever done that for me before.

Dan groaned. "You saying I have to move to check?" A heavy sigh followed, and I chuckled.

"Afraid so," I answered, admiring his arse in his tight jocks when he got out of bed to go and look.

He returned triumphant. "Just gone seven," he said.

My grumble was immediate. "I best get up. I promised to open up at eight."

Before I could even pull the sheet back, Dan was on me, pinning me to the mattress. Deliciously heavy, his body moulded perfectly to mine. "I don't want you to go yet."

I chuckled. That was until I saw the desire filling Dan's features. If I stayed, I'd be holding his legs open and begging him to let me put that sizzle reflected in his eyes to good use. I had no choice but to shake my head. "I can't be late."

He groaned, his head lowering so his mouth could reach my neck. Heated kisses pressed against my skin, one of my many fantasies come to life. I moaned with each kiss, each scrape of stubble across my sensitive flesh. "You sure you can't just be a little late?"

A breathy "God, I wish I could" escaped my parted lips. "But with everything going on, the library has been a hub for families. We've all but got a mini day care set up, so I really can't stay."

Dan lifted, hovering above me, his groin still pressed against my own. I tried my best not to think about how hard and willing he was. "Fair enough," Dan finally said. "Can I see you tonight?"

Our gazes connected, and happiness sprang to life in my chest. "Definitely." I leaned up and pressed the lightest of kisses to his lips. There was no way I could let it go beyond that. Dan was temptation personified. Too long connected, wrapped in his heat and intoxicating presence, and I'd be lost forever.

He seemed to see my struggle as he angled off me, returning to rest back on his mattress.

I glanced longingly at him, sleep-ruffled and looking sexy as sin, and I started to question my sanity. Seemingly forever I'd waited for a chance with Dan, had lusted after him for so long, and cared about him more than any other guy. It seemed wrong to be leaving now.

"Hey." Dan's quiet voice pulled me out of my thoughts. "You all good?"

I nodded, admitting, "Yesterday feels like a dream. What if we just reacted in the stress of the moment?" *What if you made a mistake?* The thought hovered at the edges, but I stopped it from spilling out. I'd convinced myself Dan's actions over the last few months had been about letting me down gently, his careful way of letting me know in no uncertain terms he wasn't interested.

Yesterday had changed all of that. It was all so fast, my emotions, and what I thought I knew, were struggling to pull everything together and make sense of it all.

Wide-eyed, I floundered and grunted as Dan moved as quick as a red-bellied black to grab my waist and tug me back to bed. I landed with an oomph.

"You're talking crazy." Determination settled in his eyes. "We know each other too well to screw around, screw this up." His brows rose as if in challenge, and I nodded. I had no desire to fight him on any of it. All I needed was to be certain that he had no regrets. "We're going to see where this goes and have fun exploring it, yeah?"

I sighed into his hold, replastering myself against him as I inhaled the man who I wanted more than anything. "Okay, I like the idea of that. But clarify 'fun.'"

"Fun means we enjoy being together, and only together, and we make this work as best as we can."

I watched him carefully, trying to ignore the sensation of his warm hard flesh pressed against mine. He was distracting in the best of ways, but there was something I needed to know. I needed it spelled out for me, to be certain.

"So you definitely want to be more than friends."

I expected perhaps a huff of laughter, a swivel of his hips to emphasise the hardness I felt against my thigh. Instead, seriousness drew Dan's brows together. "I've wanted us to be more than friends for a long time."

"You have?"

Tenderness seeped into his eyes. "Definitely. You know what happened with my ex."

I did. The knowledge had led me to interpret his story the way I had. "You're worried about Craig." The statement sat heavily between us.

"Not about him not being on board with us being together," he said quickly, surprising me. But I filed that information away for another time. "More like if things went wrong—"

"You'd be left with no one," I cut in, my heart aching.

A slight nod was his answer.

The heavy pounding of my heart hammered with every syllable as I said, "So perhaps we go forwards expecting this, us to work out." Dan was worth the embarrassed flush heating my skin, worth me putting myself out there and perhaps being the boldest I'd ever been.

The catch in his breath caught me off guard. While Dan was sweet and caring and showed me so much warmth that he was as good as any heater, there was a vulnerability in that one reaction I'd never seen before. "Okay." The whispered word flowed over me, and my heart leaped with a joy I'd been worried to embrace.

Firm arms wrapped around me, and I smiled, content.

"I can't believe I'm saying this, but I don't think we should fuck too soon."

Disbelief and amusement had me pulling away and staring at Dan wide-eyed. "Are you serious?" I didn't know if I was referring to the sweet declaration to the shift in topic about fucking, or the fact he was saying we should abstain. Quite possibly both.

A pained expression settled on his face and he nodded. "I know, right? I'm questioning my sanity too, but if we fuck on day one and for some messed up reason, it's clear this isn't going to work..." He sighed before continuing, "I'm not sure how'd I'd get over the memory of you being in me."

I was tempted to argue that we'd just talked about making it work while he was thinking about us failing, but I held my tongue. What he said made some sense, I supposed. As painful as it was for me to admit it. And then there was the expectation of me being buried inside him. Fuck, I was good with that.

His stare was searching, and I thought testing the waters. In our years of knowing each other, we never talked about our dating lives. We certainly didn't talk about how we liked to have sex.

My gaze softened. This uncertain side of Dan was alien and all levels of sexy, making his suggestion even more difficult. But reluctantly, I bobbed my head in understanding. "I get it. I've wanted this, *you* for so long." I stroked his cheek, clarifying, "To be inside you."

His eyes sprang wide before a self-satisfied smirk passed over his lips. "Just how long?"

"Never mind," I responded. "But a little longer won't kill me, I suppose."

"Might give us blue balls," he said, and just like that, the tension shifted to something more familiar.

"What?" The word came out startled. "You never said anything about not jacking each other off or blow jobs." My cock throbbed at just the thought of his hot mouth on me.

A strained look filled his features. "How about handjobs but no sucking cock?"

"I'm not sure I'm down with that," I said, following up with an amused laugh.

"What?" Dan said, grinning.

I shook my head. "I can't believe we're talking about this and hashing out our rules of engagement."

His grin remained wide. "Me neither, but we need to do this right." Certainty weaved in his voice. "And no BJs, as seriously, Ross, the thought of tasting you...." He groaned and closed his eyes. He smacked my arse. "Okay, I need you off me now before I change my mind."

I considered screwing with him, stripping off and grinding all up on him, just for shits and giggles. But that he'd been the one to come up with these rules was surprisingly sweet. Holding back was a big deal. I understood that. Reluctantly, I moved off the bed, knowing I'd respect his effort.

He watched me stand and gather my things. His focus on me sent my heart into overdrive. I had no idea how long this bright idea of his would last, but I hoped it wouldn't be too long. I wanted him so badly I could barely think straight.

"I'm heading home to get changed," I said, leaning down and capturing his lips with mine. Dan sighed against my mouth, and I pulled away so I could focus on his expression. Warmth filled his features. My own shone back at him, and I considered just how natural this felt between the two of us.

There were no freak-outs.

No hiding.

Our kisses and touches were natural, and I wasn't sure I'd ever tire of them.

"How are you getting to work?" His car was still at my folks' place. Immediately I thought about yesterday. I'd call my parents as soon as I was in the car to check in on them.

"I'll sort it. Don't worry."

"Okay. If you see my parents, make sure they're really okay and not bullshitting, will you?" I asked.

Dan nodded. "Of course I will. They know they can't get anything past me."

I smiled at his certainty, knowing he was also likely right. "I'll call you when I've finished work to see where you are, what you want to do, okay?"

His work-roughened hand cupped my cheek. My breath caught at the tenderness. "Okay. Have a good day."

I gave him one more kiss before saying, "Try to get more sleep, and I'll see you later."

I then got in my vehicle, contemplating how incredible it would be if this thing between Dan and me turned out to be the real deal.

14

DAN

THE LATE AFTER-LUNCH START WAS A GODSEND. I wasn't sure I would have been able to get up at the same time Ross had. The past few weeks, days, and especially the past thirty-six hours had all but brought me to my knees.

But things had finally calmed. Fires had eased. Every one of us who donned our firefighting kit on top of our day jobs remained vigilant, and while another call could come through, the anticipation had dwindled just slightly.

I looked at the time. It was almost five thirty, meaning I could head home.

I'd been in the workshop today working on some cabinets. Usually, I was out and about fitting kitchens, but my late start had thankfully held me back, so I'd had a fairly easy day.

After packing up my equipment, I swept the floor before heading to grab my things.

With only Jacko around, I was able to say a quick goodbye and leave.

Craig was already waiting to take me out to his parents' place to collect my truck.

It was still plenty early enough that I'd see if they needed any help before I hightailed it out of there. The pull to spend some time with Ross made me pick up my pace. Unfamiliar nerves settled in my gut as I opened Craig's car door and sat in. While everyone yesterday had seemed okay about Ross and me, after a night to sleep on it, there was always the possibility that now the adrenalin from the fire had passed, so had their acceptance.

I had no plan to raise the subject, though.

Before long, it would be the norm for our friends and family to think of Ross and me together, but I also craved normality too. The last thing I wanted was things between Craig and me to change.

"Hey," I greeted, throwing my bag in the back seat and then tugging on my seat belt. "All good?"

Craig nodded, a yawn following. He shook his head as he pulled out of the car park and laughed.

"Yeah. Still knackered. Feel like I could sleep for a week. You?"

"Same, pretty much. I managed to get some sleep till eleven this morning. Another early night though, tonight. My body's shagged."

"I hear you." He indicated to turn right, eyes remaining on the road.

"You spoke to your parents today? Everything okay?"

"All good, thank Christ. A couple of hours after we left, the few smoulders still around were put out. And there's no damage to the buildings. The land's going to need some work. A few fence posts replacing, but in the grand scheme of things, they're helluva lucky."

"Agreed," I said. "Just let me know when you need a lift with the fencing."

"Thanks, mate. A few weeks should do it, I think. Give the old man time to source the posts. Not sure any of us have the energy to be cutting down the stringy oaks and making our own."

I huffed out a relieved breath hearing that. If needed, I'd help out and spend time felling and stripping trees and then assist cutting them up into posts, but it was back-breaking work that I'd happily avoid if possible.

"You spoke to Ross today?"

Not willing to be anything but honest with the guy, I answered, "Not since he left my place for work this morning." I side-eyed him, looking for a reaction. Relieved that just a small head bob followed, I relaxed a little.

Craig was my best mate; as such, I should have known he wouldn't be a prick. I chastised myself for remaining wary earlier. He'd said what he'd needed to say last night and even a couple of months back. Gave me his thoughts, his warning, and that was that. It was one of the many qualities I liked about the man.

"He may be at Mum and Dad's," Craig said, his words causing my stomach to flip over in expectation.

We'd said we'd contact each other after work, and that had been my plan once I'd picked up my truck. Getting to see Ross earlier than expected sounded like a win to me.

"Great. Save me a call," I said. "The less time I have to talk on the damn phone, the better."

Craig laughed, hating making phone calls as much as I did.

We spent the rest of the journey shooting the shit, making the kilometres speed on by. Before long, we were bouncing down the pot-holed driveway. Compared to when I'd made this journey yesterday, I was a whole lot calmer. The only similarity being my heart still threatened to pound out of my chest at seeing Ross.

When I saw his Hilux parked out front, I didn't even try to hold back my smile.

I was the overeager fool who all but dove out of the Toyota as Craig hit the brakes, my feet taking me to the front porch where Ross had appeared and was currently heading down the wooden steps towards me.

His grin was wide, happiness etched on his face.

"Hey," he said in greeting as my feet ate up the gravel, and I found myself in front of him, placing the barest of kisses on his lips. It was as chaste as I could get, not willing to freak his whole family out.

As I pulled away, I smiled. "Good day?"

He nodded, gaze roaming my face. In my peripheral vision, I saw movement and edged away from Ross, moving to his side when my focus shifted to his mum.

"Hey, Harriet." I walked on over and up the steps, greeting her with a kiss on the cheek, so very aware that I held Ross's hand the whole time.

"All good?" Her eyes roamed my face, concern dipping her brows low. "You look beat."

"I'm all good, Harriet. Nothing a weekend of sleep won't fix."

She didn't speak for a moment, her eyes then travelling to my hand that clutched her son's. "I made you a pie to take home for dinner. Come on in and grab it."

I grinned, squeezing Ross's hand, and followed her inside.

"Where's Dad?" Craig asked, coming up behind us.

"Out in the far east paddock. He should be back soon."

"He need me to head out to help him?" Craig asked as he stood at the kitchen window, peering out.

"Don't think so, love. He'll let you know if he does when he gets back." Harriet then busied herself, and I turned my attention to Ross.

"Your day been okay?" Just being so close to the guy, his hand still snugly held in my own, was something I could hardly believe was real. I wasn't a swoony guy at the best of times, but Ross brought out a side of me that no one ever had before. Perhaps it was having crushed on him for so long that made the difference, me knowing the man all but inside and out. But from the moment we shared our first kiss just yesterday, I readily admitted that I wanted to spend all my time with him.

"Yeah," he said, "not too bad at all. Still busy, as we're offering support to help entertain the kids while all of this nightmare is going on, but it's good to feel like I'm contributing, you know?"

"I get it."

"Here you go, Dan. One beef and potato pie for you." Harriet placed the huge pie in front of me, and my eyes widened at the size.

"Bloody hell, just how much do you think I eat?" I threw her a wink.

She quirked her brow at me. "Don't sass me, boy. I'm assuming you're sharing it with that hollow-legged kiddo of mine." Her attention flicked over to Ross, and I snorted.

"I do not have hollow legs!" Ross's protest was drowned out by laughter.

Craig, being the smart-arse he was, added, "Like shit you don't. You eat more than me."

"Whatever," Ross said, rolling his eyes at his brother. "You're just jealous you have to spend time at the gym getting fit while I look effortlessly hot."

I glanced at Ross, smiling because he really did look hot. His body was strong, arm muscles defined enough to make me drool. There was no six-pack in sight, and I was more than happy with his softer stomach and the trail of hairs I'd salivated over last night and this morning when I'd let my fingers have their fill.

"Piss off, turd," Craig shot back, earning a clip around the ear from his mum.

Craig grumbled under his breath, rubbing at his ear, and I shook my head at the both of them.

"Noticed you're keeping your mouth shut," Craig aimed at me.

I simply shrugged, more than aware there were times in the past that I'd jump in on the ribbing. "Seemed like you had this one handled," I said, a grin on my face.

Ross returned my grin while Craig groaned. "And so it begins. Dick whipped." He ducked and shifted quickly, narrowly avoiding another smack from Harriet.

"On that note," Ross said, "you okay if we head off, Mum?"

"You guys go for it. We'll call if we need you."

Ross let go of my hand when he headed to Harriet and engulfed her in a hug.

Not long after, I pulled up outside my place, Ross behind me in his Hilux.

I waited for him to exit before going inside, eager to give him a proper greeting. I didn't have to wait long. In a few steps, he was in my arms, his mouth connecting to mine, the two of us pressed together so close the heat from him embraced me.

This was no feathery-light kiss.

When his mouth moulded against mine, I groaned at the connection. Warm tongue, perfect lips, and just the right pace, and I held him close, my mouth moving against his.

A not-so-gentle tangle of his tongue against mine, and my whimper broke free, wanting more, eager for the connection, desperate for his mouth to stay on mine, on my skin, anywhere I could get it.

With my cock perking up and the bittersweet memory of the agreement we'd made earlier this morning front and centre, I knew I had to slow this down.

It didn't matter how much I was already regretting my commitment to take this slow.

When I leaned back for breath, a goofy grin on my lips, I didn't give a damn that my happiness was so transparent. "Hey," I said, my goofiness continuing.

Ross beamed at me. "Hey, back." He placed a small kiss on my lips before angling back. "You look knackered." Despite his smile, concern had his brows dipping. "You sure you're okay with me being here tonight?"

I tightened my grip on his waist. "I'm definitely good with you being here. An early night wouldn't hurt, but that can be with you."

"An early night sounds very doable," he said, his soft smile doing all sorts of things to my insides.

"Good." I bobbed my head, brushed one more kiss against his lips, and reluctantly released my hold on him. "Let me just put some veggies on to cook before I jump in the shower."

We headed into the kitchen, and I rummaged through my fridge.

It didn't take long to pull the veggies out to eat with the pie. I took a quick shower while Ross prepped it all. By the time I headed back to the kitchen, he was straining the broccoli.

When I stepped up behind him, I placed a kiss on the back of his neck. The gesture was instinctive. "Smells good," I said, wrapping my arms around his waist, wondering how I'd managed to go so long without allowing this to happen.

Fuck, I'd been a dick to hold back for so long.

Fear was terrifying and visceral, the thought of losing my friends holding me hostage. But the idea of not having this joined a whole other league of dread. I was finally realising having the chance to give this a go with Ross was worth the worry and anxiety.

How could it not be when we fit so well?

Unaware of my musings or the reason for me tightening my hold on him, Ross simply sighed into my touch. "That's all down to Mum's pie."

It took me a moment to catch up, my mind focussed on thoughts of Ross rather than the scent filling my kitchen.

"She does make a good pie."

"She does that," he said, indicating he was ready to dish up.

I shifted back, giving him space, and collected the plates.

"Where do you want to eat?" he asked, slicing the crusty pastry.

"In front of the TV all right? Could put a show on and chill."

Ross smiled. "That sounds good. My backside needs cushion time."

I snorted and made my way to the lounge, sitting and switching on the TV. "What do you want to watch?"

"Movie rather than a TV show that I'm going to get hooked on. I don't have the energy."

"Good plan." I did a quick search and selected an old action movie, not expecting to see it through, too bone-tired, but I'd give it a fair go. And with Ross snuggling up against me, I was beginning to think I could definitely get used to quiet nights in with him. It would be my aim to make it happen as often as possible.

15

ROSS

The next couple of weeks were as blissful as they were exhausting. Dan and I spent pretty much all our free time together, usually sharing a meal, chatting, and watching something on TV before we headed to bed. And it didn't matter whose bed that was. His or mine.

Life in Queensland had started to finally calm down. The devastation the fires left was terrifying, but one thing I was sure of was we'd bounce back.

We always did.

The storm promised had hit, bringing with it heavy downpours. After five days or so of unrelenting rain, it had finally stopped, helping saturate the ground. Sunshine had followed, along with the joy of mozzies and the welcome signs of green grass.

Already my cows and goats were happier.

After a few days of dry, the rain had started once more, the norm for our Queensland summers.

There wasn't a chance we'd complain about the rain, even though we were on day four and it shifted between torrential to mildly soggy. Our water tanks were filling, the paddocks no longer looking like cracked land.

I expected the small creek to rise and block off that exit at the end of the road, but I welcomed every single drop. Flash floods were a given; it just seemed a big switch from terrifying fires and drought to more water than some of our dams or the creeks could take —or that would be the case if the rains continued.

In the wake of the fires was also the clean-up, the rebuilds, which led us closer to the start of the school year. Kids were due back next week, which meant staff had a week of respite in school preparing for the year ahead.

Dan had left my house early this morning, dotting a kiss on my mouth and wishing me luck on my first official day back. I smiled at the memory, an extra lightness in my step as I unlocked the library door and switched off the alarm.

It was only seven thirty, and I didn't expect many other staff to be in until at least eight before the official start of training and preparation at eight forty-five. Being in early meant I could get ahead. I was running a session with the new staff at eleven, showing them the various systems for library use, the booking system, and the range of facilities we had on offer.

My aim was to not bore anyone to death. I knew full well the teachers were keen to get in their classrooms and spend their time planning, and today and Thursday were the main days they could get the majority of that done since tomorrow and Wednesday were the more intense mandatory training days.

I was always relieved as hell that I didn't need to participate.

In the middle of unpacking a few of the boxes of books and stationery I'd ordered, I looked up when the door opened. Alec stepped through, shaking off the rain and throwing me a huge grin. Looking bronzed and relaxed, he was the picture of a PE teacher still in holiday mode.

"Hey, hey, Rosco. How was your break?" He reached out and shook my hand in greeting.

"Yeah, bit busy and crazy towards the end there, but I managed some downtime."

He nodded, his face turning serious. "Yeah,

heard how close it was. I feel a bit shit that I headed over to Bali for most of the break. Just flew in two days ago. Everyone okay?"

"Yeah, no local injuries. Some damaged property, but nothing we can't manage, you know?"

He nodded. "Yeah, I get it. That's a relief."

"It is that." My smile was back when I asked, "So, Bali, everything okay in the end? Have a good time?"

"And some," he said, a salacious grin on his face. He looked thoroughly pleased with himself—his blue eyes bright, his slightly offset nose from too many breaks playing footy peeling slightly.

I rolled my eyes at him. "Do I want to know?" I asked, getting back to unpacking the books as I waited for him to respond.

"Probably not, but I can tell you over a few beers tonight." He wriggled his brows up and down.

With a shake of my head, I snorted before answering, "Actually, I already have plans. Perhaps tomorrow?" Dan had already said he'd make dinner tonight at his, and I didn't want to change my plans, not when a meal was followed up with the best dessert going.

"Huh," Alec said, narrowing his eyes at me. "Hot date?" This was a typical question from him when I blew him off for meeting up for drinks, but it was usually said with jest. This time though, he must have read something in my expression, perhaps heard something in my voice that lent to a more serious phrasing of the question.

I considered dragging it out, winding him up a bit, but I couldn't be arsed. "Yeah," I answered, "I have."

"You have?" His eyes were wide. The shock on his face quickly morphed into interest as a small smile settled on his mouth. "You have been busy, Rosco. Tell me more."

I rolled my eyes at him. "Dan, my boyfriend." I worked hard at containing my blush, feeling a bit idiotic at calling Dan my boyfriend. It was a term I always associated with being a kid, a teenager.

"Holy crap, Dan Madison?"

My skin heated as I nodded. "The one and only," I said, trying to distract him from my heated cheeks.

"About damn time," he said. "Good on ya."

That was the thing with Alec, despite his hyper-masculinity—the guy was the poster boy for straight, muscular PE teacher who'd earned a gold star for bed-hopping—his heart was in the right place.

He was also a good friend.

When I'd returned home after my three-year

stint at uni and my five years at a school library down south, I'd managed to land this job, which was pretty damn lucky as we didn't have that many high schools close by.

And seven years ago, when I'd started at Mitchell Oak High School, Alec had begun at the same time. It had been a quiet year for newbies, just the two of us guys and one new female staff member. And while I wasn't a teacher, we'd simply got on, despite being so different in so many ways.

As such, he knew exactly who Dan Madison was, even before Dan had returned home. Though since he wasn't exactly surprised by my news, maybe he'd known exactly what Dan had meant to me too.

Perhaps I hadn't mastered my game face as well as I'd thought.

He'd never called me out on it, though.

"Definitely beers tomorrow night with that news."

I grinned. "Sounds good. You need something or you just saying hi?"

"Hi, but also, did you hear about the new maths teacher who started?"

"Other than there being a new maths teacher, no. Why?"

"A local boy, apparently. Thought you'd have the dirt on him."

With my interest piqued, I asked, "Oh, okay. What's the guy's name?"

"Nick Smith. Know him?"

If there'd been an old-school record player playing anywhere in the vicinity, it would have come screeching to a halt.

"You're shitting me?" My voice didn't sound like my own, immediately grabbing Alec's attention.

"That doesn't sound like a good surprise. Spill?"

Tensing my jaw, I gave a miniscule shake of my head. Gossiping wasn't my mission in life, and the shit I could share about Nick Smith would have swayed Alec's reaction to the guy completely. The Nick Smith I knew was a homophobic, bullying shit for brains.

I'd been fifteen when I'd come out. It hadn't been exactly pretty, but with Craig and Dan a couple of years ahead and still at school, they had calmed the impact of threats and vileness. When they'd left, it was just the one group of wankers who'd made it their personal mission to be damn right vicious in their attacks. And Nick had been at the centre of it.

Okay, so there was perhaps some exaggeration

there. Not once had I been beaten up or anything so violent, but to my sixteen-year-old self, life for that one year before Nick left school was hell.

"We didn't exactly run in the same friendship circle," I settled on. I'd share with Alec the truth should Nick turn out to be as much of a prick now as he was way back when, but for now, I'd keep the history to myself to see if the man was able to redeem himself at all.

But based on the random exchange I'd had with his old school pal Jamie a few months earlier, I wouldn't hold my breath.

People changed. I'd seen it on more than one occasion. I could only hope the same could be said about Nick Smith.

"Hmm." Narrow-eyed, Alec studied me. There was little doubt I was holding back. "In that case, I'll check him out for myself. If there's an issue, I'll make him join the staff dodgeball team."

I laughed, my tense shoulders relaxing. Alec seriously was a good guy and had my back. "I'm on board with this plan." A quick glance at the time told me I had to get a move on. Alec followed my line of sight, sighing.

"Urgh, staff meetings and training days, oh how I loathe them."

"I'll save you a seat at the back."

"You better. You don't want me to put you on the opposing team in dodgeball. You know I'll own your arse if that happens."

My brows shot high, my smirk immediate. "Is that so?"

Alec rolled his eyes and shot me the finger. "I'll just go grab a coffee and will see you in a few."

I watched him go, my thoughts turning to Nick Smith.

A lot had changed since high school.

If the arsehat of a boy had grown to a man who still couldn't handle knowing anal sex was hot as fuck, then I'd happily remind him those were his issues, and he needed to get over himself.

My life didn't have room for bullies or prejudiced pricks. I was prepared to step up and let him and anyone else know that, should I need to.

As soon as Nick entered the meeting, I tracked his movement. The years had been good to him. Back in the day, he'd been the whole package— good-looking, on the footie and swim teams, got good grades. It was a pity all of that had been wrapped in bigoted beliefs.

He'd also been arrogant as hell.

He took a seat next to Loraine, the head of the maths department, and chuckled about something she said. My view was broken by the return of Alec.

"Cheers, mate." He angled towards the empty chair by my side.

"No worries."

"You spoke to the dude yet?"

"Nope."

"Huh, well, let me know how that goes."

I didn't respond. I simply rolled my eyes at Alec's reaction to me not being keen on the new addition to our school.

"The bloke's married."

I shrugged, not at all surprised. There had always been a girl on his arm, a pretty girl who he was dating.

"If someone married him, he can't be that bad, right?"

I snorted in response, and Alec chuckled. We both knew he was full of shit. Over the years, we'd met plenty of staff who were dickheads *and* married.

Our laughter eased off once Jacob, the principal, led the welcome meeting. Immediately I opened the book on my lap and blocked Jacob out. There was nothing wrong with the guy, but I knew he'd be saying the same old thing—talking about goals and ethos and the wonders of the pedagogy.

It was times like these I was pleased I'd opted to restream my time at uni into that of library studies. I'd taken a couple of education modules, my plan to teach English. Still, after my first placement of observation, I'd soon discovered that teaching wasn't, nor could ever be, my passion.

While I liked running some sessions with the students, being in front of the class with thirty kids while inspiring and keeping them in line was not my destiny. Instead, as a school librarian, I had a heap more interaction with the staff, which I enjoyed, while I also had much more filtered time supporting the kids with their studies.

It was a win-win as far as I was concerned.

A nudge at my side had me looking up. I shifted my attention from my book, frowning at Alec. His wide eyes, complete with rapid eye movements, had me moving my focus to the front of the room. Jacob's eyes were on me, a smile on his face.

I grinned back and gave a head bob as though I knew what the hell he'd said to me.

He quirked one of his brows. "In the library at eleven, correct?"

"Yep, I'll be here." My smile remained fixed, more than aware of the few grins cast my way that I'd been caught not listening and with my head stuck in a book.

It wasn't the first time, and honestly, I figured it was sort of expected from me by now.

"Great. In that case, let's break for morning tea. I'll meet with the senior management team at eleven and new staff at two. Have a good day, everyone, and don't forget the training tomorrow starts at nine sharp."

A second later, the room was a hive of activity as everyone jumped out of their seats and no doubt headed to grab a coffee and a brownie. Cheryl, Jacob's PA, made the best brownies ever and always made a massive batch for staff on the first day back.

"Come on, let's get out of here before the vultures get in first." Alec tugged at my arm, hurrying me up. He didn't need to tug twice.

"You get the brownies. I'll grab coffee."

"Deal," he said, and he moved towards the staffroom eating area while I headed to the cupboard to grab us mugs.

In no time at all, we'd inhaled the chocolate,

gooey goodness, scorched our tongues on the black coffee—apparently both of us needed a caffeine hit this morning—and I parted ways with Alec, all too aware I was meeting with Nick and the five other new members of staff.

It was like wading through quicksand with how slowly I moved. Being a grown-up sucked at times, as did rising above it and trying my hardest to give someone the benefit of the doubt.

Far too soon, I was back in the library, and thankfully, there were another few minutes to go until my session started. It gave me a chance to at least wipe off the splattering of rain that had managed to soak me despite wearing my raincoat.

I exhaled when I took in the empty library and headed into my small office space to grab my notes. As soon as my hand touched my notepad, I heard voices enter the quiet building. Inhaling and exhaling deeply, and resentful of the burst of unwanted nerves, I fixed a smile and stepped out into the main library, taking in the new teachers.

"G'day," I said as I stepped behind the main counter. "Let's head over to one of the workspaces first before I talk you through the basics and let you escape."

One of the women grinned at me, her bright

green eyes full of mirth and appreciation. "Absolutely take pity on us," she said. "I can already feel the walls closing in with information overload." She stuck out her hand once we'd reached one of the more comfortable workspaces with cushioned work chairs. "Name's Brie. I'm the new science teacher."

I shook her hand, liking her immediately. She was at least ten years my senior and had a friendly confidence about her. "Ross," I answered. "I'll try not to throw too much at you. I've also uploaded a cheat guide on the server, so if you come unstuck, just head there."

"Brilliant." She nodded and took a seat.

I turned my attention to a young guy who looked fresh from uni. His smile was pleasant and tinged with nerves. "Brent," he said. "Business." He shook my hand and quickly sat.

I deliberately focussed on the two other women, more than aware of Nick's presence, but I prolonged the inevitable. After I greeted Katie and Lisa, both new English teachers, my focus settled on Nick.

While I'd caught sight of him earlier in the staff meeting, now before me, there was the opportunity to have a good look at the man who, as a kid, was a tosser.

"Nick." I held out my hand to him, making a

decision to not play games by pretending I hadn't a clue who he was.

A tight smile formed on his mouth. He held my hand in a firm shake, surprising me that there wasn't an attempt to crush it or whatever toxic masculine shit guys like him usually attempted. "Ross." He dipped his head in acknowledgment, his eyes clear of animosity or any other emotion that I could garner.

And then he sat, leaving me both confused, relieved, and a fuckton of pissed off that after a three-hour build-up to this moment, that was it—the totality of the exchange.

Right. I cleared my throat, smiled again, and sat between Katie and Brent, which unfortunately put Nick directly across from me at the large round table.

"I work closely with every subject at least once a year," I started to explain. "Some subjects like English—" I smiled at the new members of the English department. "—I inevitably work a little more closely with." As I continued to explain my role, my link to research projects, booking systems, and the variety of curricula elements that went with it, I gradually relaxed.

The diversity initiative was my baby, though, and once I briefed them on the basics of bringing diversity in the classroom, I was a hundred percent in my element.

While I didn't altogether avoid eye contact with Nick—on occasion, I did a cursory, polite sweep in his direction when speaking—I was very much focussed on the other four members of staff.

By the end of it, I was laughing with Brie about library shenanigans, having pretty much wrapped up the session and given a brief tour of the facilities in the library, when Nick's voice pulled me short.

"So we're done, right? We can get out of here?"

Wide-eyed, I looked at him, my brows dipping low a moment later. His tone was difficult to describe, though his eagerness to get out of here, and no doubt from me, was at the forefront of his question.

"Yeah, sure." I nodded, not offering a smile. "If you need anything, just be sure to reach out to me," I directed at the group at large.

"Thanks again," Brie said. "And staff tend to gather for after-work drinks at which pub?"

I laughed. "The Big Gum right at the edge of town. Fewer students head that way, so it's the safest bet."

"Just tell me when and I'll be there. Just staff, or do people bring their other halves too?"

A flutter let loose in my stomach at the question, my thoughts immediately going to Dan. "Some do. Staff usually meet straight after school, though, which means that many partners are still working. There's always a few who stay out for longer, and then partners catch up."

"Sounds good. I know Hannah will be interested in grabbing a beer one time. It helps her put faces to names."

I glanced down at her hand, noticing a wedding ring. "Hannah's your wife?" I hedged. It was rare I'd come out with such a question, as shit as that was. Still, in the single hour I'd spent with Brie, I'd already figured she was liberal as well as smart, so if I was wrong, I didn't imagine her being offended, and if she was, I'd totally read her wrong and wouldn't even give two shits if she was an arsehole about it.

"Yeah. She's an office manager. Has just started work for a local cabinetmaker."

"Really? Bright & Sons?"

"That's the one. How'd you know?"

I chuckled, giving Brent, Katie, and Lisa a small wave goodbye as they packed up and clearly wanted to get out of here. While Nick gathered his belongings, I didn't pay him any attention. "There are a couple of cabinetmakers in the area, but Bright &

Sons is the only place big enough to need an office manager."

"Gotcha. It's her first day today. They're not a bunch of arseholes there, right?" Humour lit her words, and genuine curiosity shone in the depths of her eyes.

"Nah. They're good blokes and women. There's a couple of female fitters who work there too."

Surprise lit up her features. "That's refreshing."

"It is. Plus, Dan, my boyfriend, works there." A flash of pleasure raced along my skin when I said the words. It was heady and totally bloody awesome that I could finally say that about Dan—long gone was my awkward embarrassment when I'd said the same thing to Alec a few hours earlier. Even better was that saying the words to the woman before me came with no ill-ease or sense of dread and wonder at their reaction.

"Dan. Got it. I'll make sure Hannah knows, though I expect she'll already be knowing everyone's business by the end of the week." She grinned widely, and a shared understanding passed between us—that camaraderie, that sense of family that I still only experienced with others who identified as queer.

It was refreshing, not quite a relief, as that didn't

seem like the right word. Since my family was incredible, and I had the hottest boyfriend imaginable, I felt supported and was absolutely loved, and that was the case at work, too, for the large part. But the LGBTQ+ community in our immediate area wasn't all that visible. While I could travel forty-five minutes south and find a very different, more vibrant community, the idea of having something similar here was kinda nice.

"Shit, I have a department meeting in ten minutes. I need another coffee before that happens." With a parting wave over her shoulder, she raced away in a flurry of flowery perfume, leaving me with a smile.

Shuffling behind me made me pause.

I frowned and turned around to see Nick standing by the table. He seemed to hesitate, his gaze flashing at mine as he twisted his lips before his expression smoothed out.

"You all right there?" I asked, pleased as punch at my steady, couldn't-give-a-rat's-arse tone. "Don't you need to be dashing off?" I raised both brows at him, leaving no doubt that his earlier interruption was at the forefront of my mind.

"Yeah." He paused before he burst out with "I didn't know you worked here."

I arched a brow at him, my face beyond that one movement carefully neutral. "I clearly do."

He nodded, the gesture appearing uneasy. Colour hit his cheeks, surprising the crap out of me. Nick Smith flustered? Holy crap, hell had frozen over, apparently.

I'd seen Nick red-cheeked a time or two, but always with the high of being a mean son of a goat.

"Yeah, that's good. I'd better get going." With an abrupt turn, he hightailed it out of the library, leaving me bemused and eager for the day to already be over.

I wasn't a fan of the memories or feelings Nick evoked. The meeting, him being here, left me rattled. I just needed to find a way to deal with the uncertainty edging into my mind. Anxiety wasn't my friend. The last thing I wanted was to relapse into a version of myself I didn't like.

16

———

DAN

It was still raining heavily when I arrived at Ross's. The gravel road was already slick with claylike mud, and the collection of potholes along the access road and his drive were brown puddles.

I smiled despite the lashing rain, ease already circulating through me at being on Ross's small property.

When I'd first returned home about seven months ago, it hadn't taken me long to recognise that absence had not put a damper on my attraction for Ross. As I eased myself back into the quieter way of hinterland life, his small property became one of my favourite places to be.

I rented a small place in town, which suited me just fine when I'd relocated. Still, each time Craig had headed over to his brother's place to help out with some remodelling—or whatever Ross needed help with—I was all over it without a second's hesitation.

It quickly became the norm for me to rock up at Ross's without Craig, my attraction growing for the man inordinately. We'd always been comfortable around each other, but now, with this change in our relationship, hell, I still struggled to wrap my head around that he was my boyfriend, and we were giving this a real go.

My past relationships had been nothing to write home about—even my last disastrous one. I liked to think perhaps my subconscious tripped me up on purpose, making me hold out for Ross, but honestly, such ideas were even too fanciful for me.

All I knew and felt was Ross and I had something good going. Just the thought of him had my heart pounding that much harder and my dick thickening till I was sure a single touch would have me shooting my load in five seconds flat.

But when I was with the man—the sexy-as-hell librarian, who was so damn smart and witty and kind, and alongside all that, he still knew how to work a tractor and wrangle cows—hell, a calm like I'd never known before wrapped around me, as comforting as a spark of light in the darkness.

As I pulled up, Ross opened the front door and stood on the veranda, squinting a little through the heavy rain and the gloom of the late afternoon. Grabbing my bag and my keys, I raced to greet him and get my butt out of the relentless deluge.

"Hey," Ross greeted, hands immediately on my waist and hauling me towards him. Our mouths touched all too briefly before he eyed my damp face. "Let's get you dried off."

"Wetter, actually." I chuckled and followed him inside, tugging my rain-splattered glasses off. "I reek of work so need a shower."

Appreciation shone in his gaze when he eyed me up and down. That he'd only just noticed I was in my work clothes, I liked a lot. "I like how you smell." He took a step towards me after closing the front door. Light kisses trailed along my neck, and my dick thickened, goosebumps rising.

"You do, huh?"

"Uh-huh," he mumbled, not stopping with the kisses.

I shamelessly angled my neck, giving him better access, and clutched at his waist, nudging his crotch with mine and expelling an appreciative groan on contact.

His snort had me pausing and angling back, my eyebrow cocked.

"Sawdust is something I hadn't bargained on." He grinned, sticking out his tongue and swiping at it.

I snorted. "Shower it is."

He grinned and took a couple of steps back. "I made pizza."

"*Made* pizza?"

"Well, I bought a pizza base and threw all the good stuff on it."

"The good stuff we both like?"

His grin turned into a smirk. "Maybe. Go get the stink of work off you, and I'll throw the pizza in the oven." He turned and headed towards the kitchen, and I had no issues in watching him walk away. He was already out of his work trousers and shirt and wore the grey trackies I loved so much.

"Stink," I hollered. "So much for liking my sexy scent."

Dark eyes peered back at me from over his shoulder. That stare hit me hard, drawing forth an easy smile and an increased beating of my heart.

There it was.

The peace he evoked in me.

I had no idea how he did it: worked me up, leaving me almost panting while a comforting calm spread in my system, settling soul deep.

He didn't speak, and neither did I. Instead, unable to resist him, I took the few steps needed, clamped down on his hips, pushed against him, and kissed the back of his neck.

Ross's gasp was everything.

With every semblance of self-control I had, I smiled against his skin, whispering, "I'll be right back," before I edged away, picked up my bag I'd lost along the way, and headed to his bedroom.

It didn't take long to clean up. When I left his room, my soft shorts hugging my backside just enough I hoped it was impossible for Ross's eyes not to stray, I inhaled the heavenly scent of cooked dough and melted cheese.

"Good timing," he said when I entered the kitchen. Knife in hand, Ross sliced the pizza, cutting it into haphazard triangles.

A quick glance around the space showed me drinks weren't on the side yet. "Water, beer, or something else?"

"Beer, definitely."

I quirked my brow at his tone as I headed to the fridge. "Not a good first day back?" While Ross had spent a lot of time at the school over the summer with the fires and later doing some reorganisation or something in the library, today was the first official start of term for staff.

He grunted and placed our plates on the small kitchen table. A bowl of salad already sat in the middle, along with some cutlery and cheesy garlic bread. "No, it was okay until Nick Smith rocked up."

My eyes widened at the name I'd heard just a few short months ago; prior to that, it had been years. Needing to clarify, I asked, "From school, that Nick?"

"One and the same." He didn't look particularly pleased about it, and I immediately understood why.

Nick had been a cockhead at school. He was a year younger than Craig and me and a year older than Ross. He'd always had a reputation for being a mouthy shit, but when Ross had come out in my last year of school, there'd been a time or two Nick had started something.

Craig and I had shut down that pretty fast, but based on seeing Jamie at the Thai place, it was clear that Nick and his friends had started up again when we'd left school.

"As a teacher?" I struggled to get my head

around the odds of Nick showing up not long after we'd seen Jamie.

"Yeah. Maths."

Surprise rippled in my chest. "For real?"

He grunted a happy snort as he chewed a mouthful of pizza. "Surprised the hell out of me too."

"So what was he like?" Ross could undoubtedly look after himself. He was probably the smartest guy I knew, and there wasn't a chance he'd let anyone get away with talking shit these days, especially if they were a homophobic prick.

But saying that, even though he'd handled himself with Jamie at the restaurant, it had taken a few days for him to shake off the strange mood clinging to him. It had actually taken weeks after for us to venture out for dinner again, and while I hadn't challenged him, I suspected it was something to do with fearing a repeat of last time.

"Fine, I guess. I don't know, a bit wary maybe."

I nodded. "Understandable."

"You think?"

"Sure. I imagine the reality of what a shit he was in high school slapped him in the face pretty hard."

Tilting his head, Ross dipped his brows. "I guess you're right. If he's turned into a half-decent guy, I hope he was mortified at seeing me."

I snorted. "Don't hold back there, Ross."

A sly smile appeared. "My bitchiness is rare."

I barked out a laugh. "But when it comes out, damn, best run for cover."

He took another big bite of his pizza, the humour I was used to seeing evident in his eyes.

We settled down to eating, talking about the rest of our day. He told me about another new member of staff starting and that her wife worked at my place. The name registered immediately. I'd only briefly met the office manager this morning when I'd grabbed some paperwork.

She seemed nice enough and already appeared to know what she was doing, in as much as she knew the job I asked her about and where the paperwork was.

"I'm going for a beer with Alec after school tomorrow."

"Come to mine after?" I asked, not wanting to miss out on the chance of seeing him.

"You not getting tired of me yet?" The smile slanting across his mouth told me he knew exactly what my answer to that question would be.

"I'm tired of *not* seeing you more often."

He snorted and rolled his eyes, though he didn't

disguise his pleasure at my words. "We've seen each other practically every day."

It was true. Since that day a few weeks back, there'd been three nights we hadn't spent together. I was totally counting. Craig had ribbed me a few times about just how addicted to his brother I was. I happily took it all.

Sure, we were new, but as far as I was concerned, the six months before that had been one long game of foreplay. Admittedly, the non-touching variety, but the flirtation had been there, the desire to spend time with each other driving me to spend as much time with him as possible.

And even when I'd attempted distance, I was the first to admit that hadn't worked out so well.

"So sue me for missing you when we're not together." The sappiness just poured forth. I ignored the heat in my cheeks and focussed on the soft, warm stare Ross directed at me.

"I miss you too." He leaned in and punctuated his words with a sweet kiss. When he leaned back, there was a shift in his eyes. Heat reflected in their depths. Desire was a wonderful, heady thing. We'd made out a lot, but beyond handjobs, we'd held back.

It was different, this holding back, but fuck, it was awesome. That build-up, the anticipation. It meant when I got my mouth on Ross and had him buried deep inside me, I would relish every single taste and connection.

From the look in his eyes, he seemed just as needy as me.

His voice dipped low, saying, "You know, our going slow"—I grinned that our thoughts were so in synch—"has me all ramped up."

"It has, huh?"

"Yep." He popped the *p* and brushed his thumb over my forearm.

"So, does that mean you want me to suck you off?"

He laughed loudly, and lightness filled my chest at the absolute happiness radiating from him. "God, yes."

I stood and held out my hand. "In that case, I want you naked and on your bed, and I'm going to have a quick shower."

Ross narrowed his eyes. "You've just been in."

"Sawdust has a habit of getting into other places."

His lips twitched. "I can cope with sawdust."

Heat crept through me. I had specific plans for being in the shower. Rinsing off sweat and sawdust had been just a couple of the ministrations I'd managed before dinner. "I want to clean *everywhere*," I emphasised.

Jumping from his chair, he clasped my hand, tugging me towards the bathroom with a laugh, and all but shoved me inside.

I chuckled as he turned the shower on for me, but my laughter quickly died off when his heated stare slammed into mine.

"I'll be naked and waiting."

He kissed me as he passed me by, and I angled after him, struggling to break the connection.

I pulled away and smirked as he called over his shoulder before closing the door, "With lube!"

I grinned. There was no going slow, no gentle undressing. Naked in mere seconds, I jumped in the shower getting myself as clean as possible in my haste and doing a little prep too. While we'd only really mentioned BJs, I wasn't taking any chances, absolutely eager for more.

A couple of weeks ago, we'd already shared we were both on PrEP and tested regularly. It had been a while since I'd last fucked around—before I'd moved back to town, in fact—but I still kept up to date with all things health-related. Knowing he did the same was a heck of a relief.

Hoping he'd be sliding into me bare in a short

while had me groaning as I finished soaping myself off.

In just a few steps, I was in his room, still damp and so very eager.

Ross lay on the bed, propped on his elbows, looking sinfully delectable. I took my fill. While it wasn't the first time we'd been naked together, knowing my mouth would be latched on his cock gave me a new appreciation for the combination of lickable muscles, soft skin, and the slight thickness around his waist.

After taking my time appreciating the hair in the middle of his chest, I moved to the mattress, reached over, and stroked up his calves. Warm to touch and covered with a splattering of hair that tickled my palms, his calves were firm. Palms working upwards, they made contact with his thighs.

Ross's breath hitched, drawing my attention to his face. With his eyes at half mast like this, he looked hot as hell. The slight curve of his lips had me pausing, my own smile forming.

"You're so fucking beautiful."

Pink materialised on his cheeks at my words. I'd never called another man beautiful before, but Ross was that and so much more.

My blunt nails scraped upwards, continuing the

journey till I paused at the sensitive skin at the apex of his thighs. A groan escaped Ross's lips. My cock throbbed at the sound, my arse clamping down on nothing but air, desperate and eager for the time Ross would be planted there.

But for now, having him in my mouth, all hot and hard, would be more than enough.

"Any time now will do," Ross said, his voice gruff. Despite the neediness, he smirked.

I chuckled. "Patience. We've waited this long." And honestly, I had no idea how we'd managed it.

I wanted everything with this man.

All his smiles, his affection, his conversation, and his cum too.

"I'm over patience being a virtue." He flopped back on the bed, his elbows no longer keeping him up, eyes closing. The disgruntled sigh that escaped him had a fresh laugh escaping me.

"Yeah?" I asked, amused and so damn relieved we were clearly on the same page.

"Make that a hell yes." He peered at me, the expression in his gaze catching my breath. I swallowed hard and wet my lips, already anticipating his taste and the feel of him.

I shot a cocky half-smile his way and lowered

down between his legs, getting comfortable, having no plans to vacate this spot any time soon.

His cock was long, slender even, sending anticipation into my stomach, knowing I wouldn't have to open so wide I'd end up with jaw ache in a few minutes, but the length alone would have me working hard.

Zeroing in on his length, I took him in my hand. The desire to lick every long inch of it fluttered to life. I squirmed on the bed in anticipation, sighing at the friction against my cock.

"Dan."

I glanced at him. Need to the point of desperation had my name sounding strangled. The desire to completely destroy this man, my Ross, flooded my system in the best of ways. I'd work him over until he begged me to either stop so he could plough into me or finish him off with my mouth in the sweetest of releases.

Either of those challenges I was up for.

Rather than making him ask again, I ran my tongue over his firm length. I paid careful attention to the softness of his skin that contrasted perfectly with the steel under my tongue. After licking his glans, I paused and dipped my tongue into the slit lightly, tasting the tang of his pre-cum.

Ross's groan had me wriggling again. That sound he made could all too easily be my undoing. Eager for more of him and those groans, I opened my mouth, took him inside, hollowed my cheeks, and sucked hard.

"Dan.... Holy shit... fuck...."

A quick glance up at him while still bobbing like I was on a goddamn mission to suck his brains out. Our gazes connected. Lust-filled eyes peered at me, ratcheting up my movements.

A garbled groan passed between his parted lips at my efforts.

I gripped the base of his cock, kicking out my pinkie to stroke across his balls as I moved my hand.

Controlling my breathing, I inhaled through my nose before taking him deep, desperately wanting to test out just how long he was. His cock hit the back of my throat.

Shockwaves of heat pulsated out of me. The combination of Ross's hands now gripping my head, his not-so-gentle thrusts helping me to take him deeper was almost too much.

I was on fire.

"Fuck." Ross thrust into my mouth with jerky movements. "I need inside you."

Elation like a wave of morning heat from a beautiful sunrise caressed me.

I wanted that so fucking badly. So much so, I yanked away from him and took a deep breath.

Startled eyes peered back at me. "You okay?"

"God yes, but fuck, I almost came."

A sly smirk kicked up Ross's lips. "Yeah?"

"Just the thought of you fucking me." I shuddered, anticipation rolling along my skin.

"In that case, let's swap and calm you down before I work you back up again."

My shit-eating grin held nothing back, and Ross chuckled as I moved so quickly I almost fell off the bed in my eagerness.

"Fuck off," I grumbled with zero heat and 100 percent affection.

"How about I fuck you instead?" His quirked brow had me snorting. Ross was the epitome of kind, courteous, and professional. Pretty much a necessity considering his career. I loved that about him.

But this dirtier side—still with the quick wit and fun—was my favourite.

I didn't have time to share as much with him before my groan slipped free from the slide of his finger inside me. My eyes shot open, wondering how I'd missed him getting the lube.

"Okay?" His question was breathy.

"Definitely." I forced myself to stay still rather than greedily riding his finger. I wanted him to have the moment and take control, loving the concentration warring with desire flittering across his features. With his bottom lip tugged between his top teeth, the pink high on his cheeks, and his intense gaze on his fingers and my arse, there wasn't a chance I'd mess with the perfection of the moment.

I gasped, delight rippling across my skin after the initial intrusion of a second, then a third finger.

His attention flicked to mine in question. I smiled and nodded before groaning, letting him know I was more than okay.

"You are so incredible."

His focus danced between his fingers and my eyes, clearly not knowing where to settle.

"I can't believe I finally get to do this with you."

A flurry of activity came alive in my chest at the tenderness of his words, addling my brain and making it a struggle to form a reaction. With his fingers working me over and the awe in his voice, my balls tingled, heat licking against my spine.

"Gonna come. Get inside me." It was all I could manage, but I needed him with a certainty and desperation that left no doubt whatsoever about my feelings for Ross.

In the next breath, his fingers were replaced with his cock. He eased into me with a rightness that took my breath away.

He gripped my thighs, angling them back a little further, closer to my stomach.

"Fucking spectacular." His quiet words and unwavering stare slid over me. I groaned at the sensation of his movements and the impact of his words.

Once seated inside me, he paused, though the gentle shake of his limbs told me all I needed to know.

He wanted me as much as I did him.

I smiled, not holding back any of the affection I had for the man, hoping like hell he could read it clearly in my eyes, my smile, the way he fit so perfectly with me. I angled my head in a clear invitation. After a soft smile, his mouth was on mine.

I wove my arms around him and moved my hips while opening my mouth and kissing him with a gentleness that matched the soft thrust of his hips.

Ross rocked into me, and I groaned into his mouth.

Both of us slick with lube, Ross moved with ease. Angling up, he peered down at me, a gentle smile on his face just as he changed the tempo. My loud groan pierced the air.

I garbled something about "fuck" and "yes" and "harder" and "nailing it again" but had no idea if any of it made sense.

Though something must have hit home. Ross shifted to his knees, held on to my thighs, and snapped his hips. If he hadn't been holding on so damn tight, I was sure my head would have made a pretty hole in the bedhead, but there wasn't a chance I'd be stopping him. Not when with every snap he grazed my sweet spot, and not with the absolute focus and need shining in his eyes.

And all that emotion was unwaveringly directed at me.

Soft and gentle was long gone as we chased our orgasms.

There was nothing I wanted more than to feel his cum inside me and see mine painted over the both of us.

"Nnughhh." I groaned when Ross shifted his hips once more, nailing my prostate. It had been so damn long since I'd come from sex. Knowing how good it was to release this way spurred me on. I needed this from him. "More, Ross."

Surprise shot into me when he flipped me over.

Awe at his strength and amusement at the suddenness of the movement had me snorting a laugh. That soon changed to a whimper when he pushed back inside me with one slick thrust and continued to drill me.

This, everything Ross had to offer, I craved. Rough and hard followed by a tender caress on my back and dirty, sweetly whispered words.

He drove into me, his light moans becoming grunts. My own became desperate, demanding, and I had no fucking idea how I hadn't already spiralled. Not with just how perfect this was.

My skin heated, and I angled my head around as far as I could. His mouth clashed awkwardly with mine. The kiss was messy, desperate, needy, and clumsy as hell, but just what I needed.

Ross angled back and stared into my eyes with such fierce intensity, a new zip of pleasure tore through me.

I clutched at the pillow as a strangled moan escaped me. My orgasm hit hard, spilling out onto the sheets, and all without a single touch of my cock.

Ross grunted and tugged me up. My back pressed against his front, and he scooped his arm around my chest, holding firmly.

I jerked as the final shot of cum burst out of me,

and I writhed against him. Ross's guttural groan followed as he pressed his face against my neck. A single thrust followed before the heat of his release coated me.

I contracted around him at the sensation, feeling needy and wanting him to stay buried inside me as long as possible. Once I clamped down on his dick, another groan escaped his lips.

I tilted my head in his direction, a lazy grin forming. "That's my new favourite thing, ever."

He eased back so he could see my face. "Mine too." The sweet grin Ross angled my way had me swallowing back my emotion.

Now, with him still inside me, wasn't how I wanted to tell him the depth of my feelings.

There'd be another time soon, one where my emotions wouldn't be contorted in my sex-happy brain.

17

———

ROSS

ALEC LEANED BACK ON HIS CHAIR, WIDE-EYED, his nostrils flaring and brows scrunched. I chuckled while welcoming the hit of warmth his reaction gave me.

"The cockhead." He shook his head, his features struggling to settle on a single reaction or emotion. "I know I had my head buried in footie and pussy at high school, but I swear to God, if I'd attended the same school as you, I would have kicked his arse. What a shit for brains."

I snorted at the onslaught of images and wasn't at all surprised he'd been having sex in high school. Nor was I surprised he put footie above women. He wasn't quite that bad since I'd met him, or at least not as bad today as he was seven years ago, but he didn't seem to have any intention of settling down anytime soon.

"Aren't you a regular knight in footie boots." I followed up with a grin, and he lost some of his vexation, offering me a smirk. "I didn't tell you any of this so you'd start shit, though. It was a hell of a long time ago." I'd folded and told him about Nick. I couldn't not, as this was Alec, who was as relentless as a hard-on determined to say hello when watching *Magic Mike*. He'd checked up on me a ridiculous number of times today about the new maths teacher and made it clear he wouldn't let me leave the bar till I dished the dirt.

"I'm not going to go and kick the shit out of him or anything." Alec rolled his eyes. "Give me some credit."

I stared at him, unblinking.

"I was thinking more of screwing with his coffee, sweet-talking Angela who organises the timetables that he's first pick for cover if someone's away." Alec looked far too pleased with himself as he took a swig of his beer.

"That sounds awesome and all, but no. He hasn't mentioned it, and that's fine. I just want to put it behind me."

Nick being here had sent me spiralling yesterday,

but today... after last night with Dan, fuck, my past and Nick barely registered on my radar.

The memory of being buried in Dan, of his mouth wrapped around my cock, yeah... those memories were absolutely worth the energy and investment.

"Seriously?"

"Yep. I already had... put it behind me," I clarified, obviously not going into details about what filled my brain instead. "His crap behaviour back then has no impact on who I am today." That was never clearer to me than right now. Last night had been the perfect night with Dan, effectively changing a weird day with my anxiety brewing to one of absolute perfection.

This morning I'd woken early to loud rain on the tin roof. Rather than finding sleep when I'd curled against Dan, restlessness had kept me frustratingly alert. Thoughts of Nick being back crawled into my brain when I'd thought about the day ahead. But then Dan made this weird snore-snort sound. Immediately distracted, the only thoughts consuming me had been how long it would take for Dan to wake up with my mouth on his dick. Less than seven seconds, apparently.

Alec huffed out a sigh. "You're no fun."

"Right. And here's me trying to make sure you don't get your arse fired."

"I'll shut up if you go and get the next round."

I smirked at him, shaking my head. "My round anyway."

As I stood, movement at the entrance drew my attention. On cue, my heart managed an impressive backflip, and those telltale wings took flight in my stomach. My grin was immediate.

I changed route and took the few steps needed to reach Dan. He leaned in and gave me a chaste kiss, not giving a shit that we stood in the middle of the bar.

There was little doubt locals knew both of us were gay before this moment, but Dan's greeting cemented the deal. Sure, I'd come out when I was younger, but I'd only been out for another man when at uni and at my first job. For seven long years I'd been here, and I'd had a few discreet hook-ups with a couple of staff who were now long gone, but nothing serious and nothing public.

"I didn't know you were coming?" I said, my gaze roaming his face. It had only been about nine hours since I saw him, but that didn't deter from how much I'd missed him.

"We finished up early, so thought we'd come and join you."

My mind caught on "we." My attention shifted to his right, landing on my big brother. Craig's arms were folded, his right brow quirked high.

"Good of you to notice I'm here too." He tutted at me. "You can buy me a beer to soothe my hurt feelings."

I snorted. "Right, hurt feelings. Is that what we're going for?"

"Yep. You know what I like. I'll go wait with Alec."

He left us to it, and I headed to the bar, Dan at my side.

"You don't mind me crashing, do you?"

"No," I said immediately. "It wouldn't be the first time you guys have joined us for a drink." Even before Dan came home, Craig used to hang out. He'd become decent mates with Alec over the years too. The two of them occasionally went out by themselves when looking to hook up, which I fully supported. Before I'd introduced them, Alec had been foolish enough to ask me to be his "wingman" or some such nonsense.

It didn't take him long to figure I was lousy at it.

"Yeah, but this is different now, right, with us being together?"

The question was there in the lilt of his voice, and a look of uncertainty flashed in his eyes.

I smiled softly and reached out and took his hand while we waited at the bar to be served.

"It doesn't have to be different. We still hang out, have fun. The difference is you get to take me home." I leaned in closer and beckoned him to follow suit so I could whisper close to his ear. "And I get to make you scream out all those dirty words to me."

Dan jerked his head away so fast he almost clipped my nose. "You want to skip the drinks and go and do that now?" His pupils were dilated, his breathing shallow.

I grinned, loving that I had this effect on him. That balance, how we had the power to turn each other inside out, was a hell of a thing.

"What'll it be, Ross, the same again?"

I jolted at the sound of Ben's voice. Clearing my throat, I offered him a smile while wondering if my face was glowing red or not. "Yeah, thanks, Ben. Plus a Great Northern and a Fifty Lashes, please."

"On it."

Ben walked away and Dan groaned beside me.

I glanced over at him and smiled. "Just one beer and we're gone."

He narrowed his eyes at me. "One beer, no matter what either of them say."

Amusement flashed, thick and fast, understanding exactly what he was talking about. There was no doubt both Craig and Alec would bitch about us leaving after only one more drink.

A few minutes later, we set the drinks on the table, and Dan grouched at my brother. "Stop being an arsehole and move."

Craig's eyes were wide, his ability to feign innocence not working. "What? I left you two chairs." He looked at either side of him and the two empty chairs.

Alec chuckled. "You never had a problem before with seating arrangements."

"Don't you bloody well start." Dan shot him a look that had Alec laughing louder and raising his hands in front of him. "Just saying."

"Fine. I'll sit here and Ross can sit on my lap."

I laughed. "Uhm, no... Ross can't sit on your lap." I rolled my eyes and sat down, luxuriating in the happy flutter in my heart that Dan was needy.

"Bloody hell. You're just gonna sulk if I don't let you sit next to him, aren't you?" Craig said, shaking his head at Dan. "This is going to take some getting used to."

Dan shrugged, then grinned when my brother moved. I watched on and focussed on my brother.

I believed him when he said he was happy for Dan and me. Still, I didn't want this to impact his and Dan's relationship, especially as I understood part of Dan's reluctance to start anything up with me was because of concern about a friendship fallout. They'd been best friends forever, even when Dan left for a different pace of life for a while, so I couldn't imagine that happening.

Dan took my hand in his and pulled my attention away.

"You okay?" He dipped close to ask.

"Yeah. Just thinking is all."

"About?"

I shrugged, not wanting to open this up for discussion. But I would have a private word with my brother when I got the chance. While I didn't need to clear the air, I wanted to check in on him and perhaps offer my own reassurances. "Nothing important. Honest." I'd tell him later that I'd chat to my brother. Keeping it a secret was unnecessary, but that could wait till we were alone.

"Okay." He accepted my response readily, and I squeezed his hand in thanks.

"Is that still the plan?"

I'd barely been listening to my brother, so I simply raised my brows and shrugged at him, earning me a sigh.

"Australia Day," he clarified.

"Oh, right. Well, if this rain carries on, I can't imagine the fair being able to take place, or at least not in its same format."

Every year, the region put on a big celebration for Australia Day. It started with poetry and stories from local Elders in the showgrounds, and a big breakfast. After that, there was a heap of indigenous activities taking place, along with family fun. The evening then finished with some localish bands, with the bar opening from six, followed by fireworks at eight.

This year was slightly different, though. The fireworks had been cancelled. The money usually spent was going into a couple of charities collecting for those impacted by the fires. And other charity-focussed events were going on too.

I knew the earlier stuff would occur in the community centre, but I wasn't sure how many bodies could fit in with the family events or music.

A couple of people on the Australia Day committee had tried to rope me in to help, and I was relieved, even more so now, considering the weather, that I wasn't involved.

"I definitely want to attend the poets' breakfast, but maybe we talk to Mum and Dad about after that having a quiet one at theirs? Put the barbie on. We can all bring a plate and drinks."

After the manic few weeks we'd had, Dan and Craig especially, the thought of a more subdued celebration held appeal.

Craig nodded immediately. "Yeah. I like the sound of that. I'll text Mum."

"Thanks." I was more than happy for him to organise that with her. "You'll come, right, Alec?"

"Deffo. And if Uncle George is doing a reading, I'll be there for the breakfast thing too. That guy is the best."

I grinned, agreeing wholeheartedly. Uncle George was an indigenous Elder and an incredible storyteller. He visited the school at least five times a year, participating in assemblies, and adding additional support to the indigenous students in our school. I had unlimited time and respect for the man.

"I might invite Brie and her wife too," I said. Today at work, she'd sat with Alec and me for lunch.

She and her wife and their six-year-old son had moved from Cairns over the summer. Right in the middle of the nightmare fires we'd been having.

They hadn't had the greatest start to moving a couple of thousand kilometres away, and they had no family or friends in the near vicinity.

I understood why some people would need a fresh start, assuming that's what their move was. But I imagined it could be lonely as hell, even as a family.

"Good idea," Alec said. "I'm interested in meeting Hannah. Just from what Brie said about her today, she sounds good fun."

I laughed. "You just want her to join the netball team."

He shrugged, not denying it one bit. Alec was a hardcore netball player on the mixed-gender team we had in town.

I'd been and watched them play a few times, and each time came away terrified and looking at every player differently. Fuck, they were scary as hell.

"I'll let Mum know. Just confirm with her if it's a yes." Craig turned his attention back to his phone.

"How about your parents?" I asked Dan. They'd been down south travelling in their caravan for months now and were heading back home. Alan and Hazel had taken early retirement a few years ago after Hazel had sold her successful business. Every now and then, they'd pop back up in town. Nobody was really sure when, or at least not until their only son returned.

"I'll ask them. They're due back Sunday, I think."

Australia Day fell on a Wednesday this year, giving us a nice midweek break.

"Did you have a busy day at work?" Dan asked me.

"A bit. No meetings today, which was a relief, but it's always manic as teachers are organising their term, sourcing books and such."

"And no issues?" His eyes held mine, waiting for my answer.

I smiled softly. "All's good. No issues at all, and there won't be."

Dan waited for a beat or two, as if taking the time to read my expression and hear the truth in my words. A moment later, he nodded. "Good. My next couple of days are going to be full-on," he grumbled. "We have to drive all the way to Hill Creek for a kitchen fit-out."

I winced. "That's a hell of a trek."

"An hour and a half each way."

"You want to come straight to mine, and I can have dinner waiting?"

Warmth bled into his eyes, and Dan stroked his thumb over the back of my hand. "That'd be great, thanks. I'll pack a bag to take with me."

I shook my head. "Pack it, and I'll throw it in my car in the morning."

"Bloody hell, you two are crazy domestic. How'd the fuck that happen so quickly?"

There was no heat in Alec's tone, only interest mixed with humour.

"To be fair," Craig answered, drawing all our attention to him, "it's been a long time coming."

I smirked, since there were no arguments from me.

"True that. For seven years I've heard about every visit that Dan made. Heard about the pining as a teenager, and these past—"

I cut Alec off with a loud laugh. "It's all lies."

"It is?" Dan said, his right brow quirked high.

Heat filled my cheeks. "Well, Alec knowing all of that is lies." I genuinely hadn't breathed a word to him about my feelings for Dan, though his tease was scarily close on the money.

Understanding bloomed in Dan's expression, making me squirm a little. "I'm happy to hear stories about Ross pining for me," my jackass boyfriend said to Alec, earning him a nudge to the ribs. He leaned away from me, laughing. "I'm sure you can come up with some creative stories, Alec."

"Not if you know what's good for you," I sassed with a quirked brow.

His laughter turned into a heated smirk. "In that case, I'll keep my mouth shut, but only if you tell me all the real stories."

"They make you want to gag, right, Alec?"

I flipped my brother off.

"You want to know how I make your brother gag, Craig? Is that what you're—"

"That would be a fuck no." My brother shuddered, our laughter swiftly following.

"Speaking of, I think it's time we get going." Dan finished off his beer, and the three of us groaned at his words while heat also hit my cheeks. "You ready?" he asked me.

"Yeah." I took the last gulp of beer, patted Alec on the shoulder, saying, "See you tomorrow," then leaned over and planted a kiss on the top of my brother's head. "Let me know what Mum and Dad say about next week. And I'll probably see you at the weekend."

Craig bobbed his head. "Will do. Stay dry."

I smiled and took Dan's hand, heading back into the pouring rain, racing for my ute. "See you at your place in five," I called out to him.

Dan nodded and made a run for his vehicle while I got into the dry.

I ran a hand over my face, wiping away the drips.

The rain was relentless, so much heavier than the front that came through immediately after the fires. It made visibility poor on the drive home. I was grateful Dan lived in town rather than out a few kilometres like me.

Before long, I pulled up outside, wishing the rental had a garage to help keep at least one of us dry, but the place was old and made of weatherboard, with no garage in sight.

Once parked, I jogged to the house. Dan was already there unlocking the door and turning the outside and inside lights on. He grabbed a couple of towels and passed me one.

"Bloody hell. It's seriously coming down," he said as he rubbed his hair.

I stared past him to the dark, wet sky. "It's forecast to slow down and a couple of days of dry after that." I squinted as I peered out. "Not sure I believe the reports with the way it's going."

Movement to my side had me circling Dan's waist. "I just hope it's dry next Monday for the first day back at school. The students are going to be feral else."

Dan offered me a smirk as we stepped out of the open doorway and locked up for the night. "And there I was wondering why you decided to change specialties and become a librarian rather than a teacher."

His words earned him a pinch on the butt.

"Come on. I need feeding," I said.

We stepped into the kitchen, and Dan pulled out the leftover risotto from yesterday. "This okay?" He indicated towards the tub.

"Sounds good to me. I'm going to jump in the shower before dinner."

He smiled, and I knew it was because he loved how comfortable I was in his space. He may have mentioned it a time or two. "I'll warm this through while you're washing up."

I stepped close and planted a kiss on his mouth. "Thanks, and thanks for coming out tonight. It was nice."

"Even though your brother gives us shit?" He quirked a brow at me.

My brows dipped low at his words.

"What's that look for?" he asked, surprise in his tone.

"You think Craig's bothered?"

He didn't even pause before he shook his head. "No. I think he's happy for us. Honestly, he's known from the moment I did how I feel about you."

My heart flipped at his words. We still had a lot to share with each other, and it seemed like this was one of many such moments I'd like for him to tell me about. "Really?"

"Absolutely." Seriousness had his focus not wavering from mine. "It sounds like he's known how *both* of us have felt for years. It's probably less of a shock for him than anyone. Even us."

I chuckled. He was probably right. I'd already figured I wasn't as stealthy in my feelings for Dan as I'd attempted to be. "I was sure you knew how I felt," I admitted.

Wide-eyed, Dan answered, "No, not at all. Perhaps I would have made a move as soon as I came home if I'd been more certain. I seemed to forever be walking that fine line of not screwing up our friendship, or mine with Craig."

"We've got a lot of history."

"And years with barely any contact," he added.

"And that's a good thing?" Curiosity lifted my

words into a clear question.

"Damn straight. It means we grew and ventured out into the world—"

"Brisbane is hardly the world," I quipped, adding a smirk for good measure.

He laughed. "Fuck off. I took holidays overseas."

His words just made me chuckle more.

"My point is," he clarified, squeezing my waist and drawing my attention back to his words, "it also means our connection... or history have kept us together in many ways, but we became adults apart, so you know, we've still got stuff, and uhm... things to learn...."

My lips twitched at his awkward sweetness, and I brushed my thumb over the patch of skin above the waist of his jeans. "You have no idea what you're talking about, do you?"

He shrugged a little, a delicious pink creeping up his neck. "I know what I mean in my head, and it sounded all right then, until I tried to put it in words." He huffed out a laugh. "I just don't want you to be concerned about Craig, is all."

I melted a little at his words and found reassurance in them. I couldn't imagine Dan ever steering me wrong. "Thank you, and I think I know what you're saying. We both had a lot of growing up to do, meaning that when we ended up back together again, we had time to reform our friendship."

"Yes, that." He bobbed his head, chuckling. "We didn't rush into this."

"Well, me jacking off to thoughts of you intermittently over the past eighteen years means there was zero rush in the making of us."

He quirked his brow. "I think you should demonstrate that soon."

"What? Jacking off?" My dick twitched at the thought of getting myself off while Dan sat back and watched.

"Hell yes. Maybe you should do it now in the shower."

"This idea of yours has merit." A twitch of my lips and I inched forwards, grinding against him, making it clear just how much I liked this bright idea of his.

My stare danced over his face. "Done, but if we're going to start following through with the fantasies I've had of you, we're going to need energy drinks." His laughter broke loudly through my words. "You think I'm joking... eighteen years, Dan." The smile that lit my face was all levels of dirty and promising, the dip in my voice a pledge he'd have no regrets getting on board with my fantasy plan.

"As long as we make room for mine too, I'm happy to oblige."

I barely finished speaking before Dan shoved the leftovers back in the fridge and dragged me towards the bathroom.

These moments right here were everything.

And with my years' worth of illicit fantasies, I had no plans to slow the pace of our relationship. Not ever.

***

"Thanks for helping me."

Dan glanced up, a smudge of oil on his face drawing my attention. There was something about him like this that made him ridiculously attractive.

Honestly, over the months before we got together, I had no idea how I managed to not simply fall at his feet and break into a Shakespearean sonnet or something, begging him to be mine.

My poetry performance voice wasn't the best, so I was relieved as hell I hadn't. To think it was the devastating fires from just a few weeks back that finally gave us both the prod we'd needed.

I still struggled to get my head around that.

It already seemed like a lifetime ago, especially

after the torrent of rain we'd been slammed with. But I knew we'd been so lucky, and other than a few of my parents' fences that still needed replacing, we'd come away unscathed.

Damn, we'd been lucky.

"No worries." Dan winked, and my heart flipped like it did so often when he was cute, or sexy, or simply breathing. "I forgot to ask yesterday if Nick had said anything to you."

Ice froze the air in my lungs, and it took a couple of beats for me to thaw them enough to catch my breath. Frustration and anxiety threaten to get its clutches into me. Each time it did, it completely confused the hell out of me, especially as my initial reaction was so quick to pass.

Shaking off my instinctive reaction when Nick was mentioned, I quirked my brow in Dan's direction. "I know I work in high school, but it's been a long time since I behaved like a high schooler." An oily rag landed square in my face for my efforts. "Hey," I spluttered with a snicker.

"That's for being a smart-arse. You knew what I meant."

"I know, but nothing, and honestly, I don't even know what I was expecting."

Nick hadn't said or done anything. The reactions

were my own, almost reflexive. Any anxiety fizzled away quickly, rational thought soon making that happen. In its place was me pissed off that this... I didn't know, defence mechanism always kicked into place.

"That's good, as long as it's not bugging you him being here."

"And if it did bug me?"

"I'm not too old to throw down."

I snorted loudly, ease loosening the tightness in my chest, and Dan narrowed his eyes at me.

"Okay, I've still got a good aim and could throw cow shit or something, maybe find out where he lives and get some local dogs to crap on his lawn." A shrug followed, amusement clear in his eyes.

"Well, aren't you just a regular vindictive hero? Be still my heart."

"Don't you forget it." He indicated for me to throw back the rag so he could continue working on sharpening the chainsaw blades.

I tossed it over. "But really," I offered, "I think just hearing his name, then seeing him threw me for a loop a little. There's been no dramas at all. He's been polite, if not a little awkward, and that's fine by me."

That year in high school had sucked. There was

no doubt about it. But long ago, I'd twisted the narrative and made it my own, knowing it had helped shape me into the man I was today.

And since I thought I was a decent bloke, my history overall had been a good one, and that time in my life didn't actually define who I was.

"That's good," Dan responded, his attention entirely on me as I spoke.

"Benji!" I interrupted, wide-eyed and peering over Dan's shoulder. "What the hell? I told you to stop doing crazy shit like this!" I threw my head back and counted to five. I would have attempted ten, but there was no chance I could risk looking away from Benji for so long. I pried my eyes open and peered through the pane of glass from my shed to the small paddock. "Shit."

I charged out, whacking my elbow on the metal door frame in the process. Wincing but barrelling forwards, I hollered as I ran, "I swear to Christ, Benji, Mrs Jameson has offered so many times to make a goat curry." I swung over the gate, only to pause at Dan's laughter.

"And exactly what are you doing?" The amusement in his voice had me smirking, despite Benji pissing me off.

"Figuring out my plan of attack."

My words made Dan laugh louder. I flipped him off, returning my attention to my goat, who was determined to drive me to distraction. "You used to be cute," I shouted at my five-year-old goat. "Now look at you. Arsehole."

Having left my hat on my workbench, I squinted against the sun's fierce rays. The rain had eased off this morning, giving me the chance to catch up with some chores this Saturday afternoon.

Benji stood tall and proud on top of the chicken coop. It was seven feet off the ground, and I was clueless about how he managed to get up there in the first place.

"I should just leave you."

Dan appeared at my side and plonked my Akubra on my head. My heart stuttered at his thoughtfulness. "You're not going to leave him." He nudged my side. "He's going to be a dad anytime now. Bessie's gonna need him."

I side-eyed my boyfriend and rolled my eyes. "You've been away in the big smoke for too long if you think that's how it works."

He chuckled. "Enlighten me then."

I shrugged. "Hell if I know. It was Mum who talked me into the bloody things, arguing they were so cute. But what goats aren't cute when they're six months old?" I sighed and focussed once more on Benji. "Now look at him. Knocked up Bessie, and rather than acting responsibly, he goes and starts doing some daredevil shit. How'd the hell he even get up there?"

Beside me, Dan's shoulders shook, not at all being the supportive boyfriend he should be.

"You know, I was so close to giving you head earlier on, thinking you looked hot in oil-stained jeans with a smudge on your face."

Dan snorted. "And I'm assuming you're even hotter for me now."

"Ha. Maybe if you get that damn goat down."

Dan's arm brushed against mine as the two of us stared at the goat on the hot tin roof. Great, now I was thinking about plays and wondering if I could think of any that starred annoying goats who thought they were stunt animals.

Benji paused his snuffling and gave an answering bleat in our direction.

"You think that's Goat for 'piss off and go screw yourself?'"

"Holy shit, I think you may be fluent in goat speak."

I hip-checked him just as another bleat echoed from around the other side of the coop.

No way.

I took tentative steps towards the sound, not wanting to give my movement away. James Bond, eat your heart out. I could be stealthy when the occasion called for it. Ross Foster didn't quite have the same suave ring to it, admittedly.

Peering around the metal sheeting, my eyes widened. Bessie stood on top of the small bin of food. Not necessarily a surprise, since my goats thought they were mountain goats rather than the cute dwarfs they were.

"Bessie, you're five months pregnant and ready to pop." I shook my head at the podgy, very pregnant goat.

Dan's voice startled me—apparently, he was even stealthier than me. "Bloody hell, she does look ready to drop anytime now. You done your research and stuff?"

"Pretty much. I've been all right with the cows. I'm hoping this is just as easy." And I seriously did.

There was little question in my mind when I moved back to my hometown a few years back that I wanted a small block of land. Moving away for uni had been good for me and helped me see this was where I wanted to be.

I didn't want a place the size of my parents' property, since I had no desire to work the land full-time. But a small hobby farm with a few animals, fruit trees, and veggies was absolutely manageable.

But I'd never been around goats before. I didn't think they could continue surprising me like this, but I stood corrected.

The sound from above had me shifting my attention.

Seriously. No bloody way.

Benji peered down at me, Dan, and Bessie.

"Unbelievable." I shook my head, my focus drifting between the two goats while wondering about Benji's ability to get on the roof. "Get your arse down here."

Benji bleated.

"Yeah, yeah." I shooed Bessie off their makeshift "stepping stool"—the metal container—and jumped up. Benji, seeming to recognise he needed to stay put for my help unless he planned to jump the seven feet, stayed in reaching distance.

"You are so going in the pot." I managed to wrangle the goat to safety and quickly shifted the container so he and Bessie could no longer check out the scenery from up high.

Task done, and no curry on the cards since Benji did have a way with the ladies by getting Bessie knocked up, Dan and I returned to my shed, pausing when his phone rang.

"It's Frank."

I nodded, focusing intently as Dan answered the station officer's call.

He paused, listening to Frank speaking. "Yeah, I've been looking at the BOM site a fair bit."

When I heard his words, I immediately realised they were talking about the possibility of flooding. Dan had read every alert that came through from the Bureau of Meteorology app. Every time it pinged with an update, he'd checked.

With how much rain we'd been having, flooding was expected. I just hoped it was the usual flash flooding on the usual creeks.

We dealt with those all the time.

Even as I tried to convince myself that would be the case, I expected different. With how much rain had pummelled us and those up north, it was a waiting—and monitoring—game to see how high the main river would rise.

"Will do, yeah. No worries. I expect I'll be seeing you soon." He said goodbye and glanced over at me. "Frank said the river's already up by five hundred mil."

"That's not great."

"Nope. You sure you don't want to head back to town with me?"

This had been a bone of contention earlier on too, when we'd headed into town to grab some fuel for my generator and a few more basics, just to cover me as it was probable the roads would be cut off.

If a flood happened, it would likely be in the next forty-eight hours or so, which was awful timing, since school was back in session on Monday.

The protocol for such events and work was if you could get in safely, with no water to cross, and your property was safe, then you were to head in. This was so parents in essential services could do their jobs knowing their kids were being looked after, especially those who had no alternative arrangements.

There was just the one major creek I'd need to cross to get into the north side of town. That creek had risen high about three times since I'd been living here, and even in my truck, I wouldn't be crossing it. Not when it was on a mission and flowing fast.

So if I were to leave, it would be soon with Dan.

But then there was the pain-in-the-butt goat who I expected to go into labour anytime now.

While I'd been brought up with the animals on

the property being absolutely livestock and not pets, I was a sucker since getting my own animals.

"You know I need to be here in case there's a problem."

Dan didn't hold back his frustration, huffing and even adding in a grumble. I snorted. "You know I'm not at risk here. I'm the one who should be doing that growly shit that you're doing, worrying about you. It's not like you'll be tucked in at home, waiting it out."

The narrowing of his eyes made me take pity on him. "Come on. Let's finish the work in the shed, then you might get lucky before I send you packing to do your heroic thing." I had to jest, to constantly make light of what he did, as well as my dad and brother. If not, my brain would make it impossible to settle whenever I knew any of them were out on a call—for fire or flood. And once my thoughts spiralled, my emotions would be quick to follow, and none of us needed that.

"You do make the best offers to get me to shut up and get off your case." Dan tilted his head and smirked. He couldn't disguise the worry dancing in the depths of his gaze, though.

I squeezed his hand, not wanting either of us to get into anything. Instead, I hauled him to the shed.

18

———

DAN

The ringing of my house phone dragged me out of my sleep. It took me a moment to figure out what the noise was. I couldn't remember the last time the landline had received a call. Admittedly I'd only been here for seven months or so, but still.... I eyed it warily, as if a dodgy salesperson was going to jump through the receiver if I answered it.

On its sixth ring, I reached out and picked up.

"This is an automated announcement by the Queensland government—"

Immediately I went on high alert, already knowing what the announcement would say. The flood warning had been activated.

I ended the call and rushed to my room to dress. My eyes snagged on the empty bed, and my heart flipped over, pissed I hadn't convinced Ross to stay over.

A quick glance at the time told me it was a little after 5:00 a.m. It was Monday morning, so the first day back at school for the kids.

That wouldn't be happening today.

It had been a long time since the Burra Bli River had flooded to the point where the town was on high alert. Sure, creeks regularly flooded, and flash flooding was a given, cutting off roads and access, but to the point of the river triggering the alarm was probably when I'd been sixteen.

A variety of creeks weaved along the south side of town, fed by the river. It would mean residents and businesses were cut off. Heading south wouldn't be possible for them, as that's where the surge of water was coming from, meaning I needed to get my arse to the station and get to work.

Adrenalin buzzed in my veins, and my hands shook as I tied my laces on my boots, then grabbed my phone.

Where my house was should be well out of any flood zone, but I took a moment to shake out my hands and take a deep breath. I quickly made my way to the circuit board, turning off the main power. I then put my laptop on the kitchen counter, rather than leaving it on the floor next to the sofa. Looking around, I couldn't see anything else at ground level I needed to worry about.

Once outside, my phone rang. Craig's name flashed on the screen.

As soon as I picked up, he asked, "You on the way to the station?"

"Yeah, just leaving now." I started my truck.

"Ross with you?"

My stomach dipped unhappily. "No."

"Fuck."

Once the riverbanks burst, he'd be isolated, cut off entirely from town, but his house was on a decent hill and a good distance from the river, so as long as he stayed put, he'd be safe.

The town had been expecting this over the past few days. Still, yesterday there'd been a heavy downpour about five hundred kilometres north, as in a few hundred millimetres in a few hours, hitting the river that fed directly into the Burra.

Despite knowing this, Ross had insisted on staying home, determined to stay put because of Bessie, his damn goat, who was due to have her kid anytime soon. Sure, we hoped the rain would ease and the river would slow, but there'd been a good chance this was going to happen.

"He'll be fine," I said, for myself as well as his brother. "He's got the generator and plenty of supplies."

"You're right. Would have been good to have him in town, is all."

I agreed wholeheartedly as I pulled away, heading to the station, flipping my phone to Bluetooth. "I'm thinking of emigrating," I said, trying to distract us both.

Craig snorted. "That right?"

"Yeah. Where's someplace that doesn't try to burn itself to ashes one moment and in the next, cover its tracks and drown us all?"

"It's all about replenishing, right?"

My own humourless snort followed. Flood was scary as hell, so different from the destruction of a fire but potentially devastating in its own right.

The positive was we'd had a warning so people could get to safety and protect themselves.

"I'm just pulling up now. You nearly here?" Craig asked.

"Yeah. Be there in two minutes." That would also give me enough time to check in on Ross before the mayhem ensued.

I ended the call and immediately called my

boyfriend. He answered on the second ring. "You okay? Off to the station?"

I smiled at the sound of his voice, allowing the tenderness evident to soothe my nerves.

"Yeah, just about to arrive. You okay?"

"I'm good. I was thinking about heading into school, though. If I leave now—"

"Hell no. If you wanted to do that, you should have stayed at mine yesterday." I threaded steel into my voice.

Ross huffed out a sigh. "Why the fuck did I come home again?"

I hmphed. "Because you can be a pain in the arse when you want to be, and that bloody goat of yours is one too." I smiled as I spoke, hoping he could hear the affection in my tone.

"Urgh. I swear, she better have this kid of hers in the next twenty-four hours."

"If not, are we going to have mutton when I come over?"

He laughed loudly. "You just might. She stole another T-shirt off the line yesterday. I expect I'll find fabric in her shit for the next week."

I snorted out a laugh, most of my tension evaporating at hearing the sound of his amusement.

"Call me if you need me, and I'll come to you as

soon as it's safe." Words we'd yet to share were at the tip of my tongue, but I wasn't sure if my worry for him pushed them to the forefront, obscuring the complete certainty of my feelings of the words, or not. I swallowed them down, needing to be sure and needing to look him in the eyes when I did tell him how I felt.

"And you be safe. No heroics, and stay dry."

"I'll try," I said as Ross ended the call. I switched off the engine and stepped out into the dry, bright morning. That was the most surreal thing. We'd had no rain since yesterday afternoon, and this morning at five thirty, the sun was already blinding, sky blue, and it threatened to be a hot one.

Yet within a few hours, it was likely the south-side of town would be underwater—just knee-deep in water if we were lucky. The two images never seemed to gel quite right.

Picking up my pace, I hauled my gear out of the tray of my truck, then headed inside for the briefing. The first thing would be finding coffee and a bite to eat. It may be my only chance for fuel for the rest of the day.

With the SES in attendance, the evacuation was so much more straightforwards. I'd never been involved with flood management before, unlike many of the other guys on our crew. While I'd done the basic training and knew the theories, dealing with so many panicked civilians was manic.

Some had already cleared out to safety. Those residents were my favourites. Many congregated at the three different evacuation points supporting those in need. Some left it to the last minute, meaning they needed extra support and ended up travelling through water that was on the cusp of being too dangerous.

Then there were the stubborn arsehats who'd refused to evacuate.

Meaning they were flooded in, trapped in their homes with a new moat accessory.

While some of the old-timers had seen more floods than I'd put out fires—and I had no doubt they'd usually be able to weather three days without mains power and such—the problem was the water was still rising.

"Apparently '76 was the last time it was this high."

I cast a look at Craig. The two of us stood

together at the edge of the new river on Mary Road. It was fast-flowing and scattered with debris.

On the other side of the street, the high-set houses were faring okay, but those just a metre off the ground would have at least that much water running through them within the next few hours if the water continued to rise, which was the prediction.

I shook my head. "Where we heading next?"

Craig pointed to the map, and I angled to look. "A big gum came down over on Avery. It's been pushed out of the water, which is something."

"A little less destruction." I nodded.

"Yeah, but it's blocking one of the access points to Degan."

"One of the main routes to the hospital."

"Yep." Craig folded his map and shoved it under his arm. "We'll take mine, since I've got the winch."

"We got the chainsaws and PPE?"

"Just need the PPE."

"Got it," I said, heading to his truck so we could go and grab the gear we needed. Once inside and navigating our way to the station, I angled a glance at Craig. "Where's your mum?"

"In town helping out at the rec centre."

"That's good." I wished Ross had done the same

and gone into school rather than been stuck out at his place.

Craig took a moment to radio out to our crew leader, letting him know we were en route. As he spoke, I focussed on the passing buildings and the seemingly hundreds of people milling around in town. Most were armed with bags or containers, all seemingly on a mission—I expected helping those impacted and assisting however they could.

Despite the loss I knew so many were experiencing, I smiled, pleased I was here to help. Small-town living called to me. In the past six weeks or so, I'd never felt that so acutely.

The ringing of my phone startled me. I tugged it out, seeing Mum was calling. I frowned as I answered. "All okay?"

"Uhm... so we may have misjudged how quickly the water was rising."

Concern slammed into me, quickly followed by guilt that I hadn't spared them a passing thought since being woken by the phone this morning. My folks had called me yesterday afternoon, letting me know they'd arrived back in town safely, and I'd therefore assumed it meant they'd hunkered down until the water had dropped.

"Where are you?"

"Your dad," Mum started—completely throwing my dad to the wolves. I would have rolled my eyes if I wasn't so worried, "thought we'd have enough time to go and grab some more fuel."

I breathed a little easier at that. "Okay, so you're in town? That's okay, you can—"

"He also thought we should get some eggs from Thomas."

I pulled my phone away and stared at it in disbelief, sure my dad wouldn't do something so idiotic. Not having enough time to count to ten, I gritted out, "Where are you now?" There'd be time enough to grouse at my dad after this crisis. "Are you safe?"

"We're okay. Over on the Bathurst Road, at the Shortskip Creek." Mum sounded pissed. I could only imagine the tension between my parents right now.

"Where's the car?"

"Stuck in the creek."

I slammed my mouth shut.

"What's wrong?" Craig asked from my side.

I huffed out a breath and glanced over at him, shaking my head. "Mum, I'm going to see who I can get out to you, okay? I'm en route to sort out a damn tree, so it'd take me at least a couple hours, maybe more, before I can get there. Just promise me you'll stay away from the creek, okay? I'll call you as soon as I can."

"Thanks, Dan. Love you."

"Love you too, Mum." I ended the call. "For fuck's sake."

"What's going on?"

"Dad's got the car stuck at the bridge at Short-skip Creek, over on Bathurst Road."

"The rest of that road doesn't flood, so that's something."

I nodded in relief, knowing Craig was right. And as far as I was aware, that creek had never been high enough to catch someone out, so it was likely it wouldn't get much higher. Christ knew how Dad managed to get it stuck.

"Get on the radio and see who's around."

"Will do, but I won't hold my breath. There's so much going on and higher priorities."

Craig winced, letting me know he expected the same. "How about Ross?"

It was my turn to wince. My protective instincts kicked in immediately. I didn't want Ross venturing out into any of this shitshow, but fuck, it was my parents. "I'll have to if I can't get anyone else."

After fifteen minutes of chasing leads, it was clear I'd have to call Ross. I needed to get a move on, though, especially as with me sorting out my parents' mistake, Craig was currently chopping a monster of a gum tree by himself.

Ross picked up on the second ring. "Everything okay?"

At the sound of his voice, I smiled, some of my tension bleeding away. "Ish," I said. "I need a favour."

"Of course. What is it?"

It took just a couple of minutes to explain about Mum and Dad and less time than that for him to figure out the safest route to get to them, one free of potential floodwater—or at least where it would be high enough to cover the road.

"I've got this," Ross said, his tone sure. "Just focus on what you need to do. I'll bring them to mine. I have the spare room."

A relieved sigh rippled out of me. "Thanks, Ross. Seriously."

"I know, and anything for you, you know that. Plus, these are your folks."

"As pain in the arse as they are, they're all I've got."

"Yep. I'll sort it. I'll call you when I've got them. If you can't answer, I'll drop you a text. Just stay safe."

The warm reassurance of Ross's voice rolled over me. He'd always been someone I could rely on, regardless of our relationship status, but now, it just seemed so much more.

Craig calling my name jerked my attention away. "Shit, I gotta go. Call you later. Stay safe. Love you." Then I ended the call and pocketed my phone, getting out of Craig's truck. It wasn't until I was pulling on the protective gear that I froze, eyes wide.

"What's wrong with you?" Craig's brows furrowed, concern in his eyes.

"I just told your brother I loved him."

"Huh. Okay." He paused as though waiting for me to clarify. When I didn't, he asked, "And that's a problem why?"

I squinted and screwed up my face, feeling like a dick. Craig's snort and following laughter had me narrowing my eyes at him.

"That was the first time, wasn't it?" I didn't even bother to nod. I didn't need to. "Ha. You dick. Did he say anything back?"

"He didn't get a chance."

Question filled Craig's expression.

"I put the phone down before he could say anything."

Craig's laugh continued as he walked away,

chainsaw in hand and finding my goof far too amusing.

Bloody arsehat.

I strolled on after him, quickly dialling Mum to let her know what was happening.

19
——————

ROSS

With Benji's bleating, it was no wonder I couldn't hear anything. Though that wasn't the reason I stood outside my shed, staring wide-eyed at my phone. Instead, it was the blood rushing in my ears, making it impossible to think straight or concentrate.

He loved me.

Then the dick went and put the phone down as though it wasn't a big deal and was something he said every damn day.

The pounding in my ears slowed. My focus shifted to my heart tripping over itself and that flip in my stomach whenever Dan did something that made my whole body want to vibrate with feelings for the man.

A smile spread across my lips.

He loves me.

My laughter sounded abrupt in the wide space, even startling Benji enough to shut him up. I shook my head, grin still in place, already imagining Dan's reaction once reality smacked into him and he realised what he'd said to me.

No matter how he handled it or played it off, this was a big deal, but hell, I wanted him to say it to my face and not almost on autopilot.

But still.

He. Loved. Me.

And there wasn't a chance I'd let him take it back.

Not that I expected he would. Even without the slip of those words, I'd hoped, maybe even expected us to be on the same page.

A loud bleat rent the air, reminding me of where I was and what I should be doing.

Dan's parents had got caught out and needed rescuing. Getting a move on, I threw a tow rope in the tray, not quite sure the condition of their car or what had really happened. I dashed to the house to collect my wallet and keys before heading over to them.

The route was set, and fifteen minutes into the

drive, everything seemed smooth sailing. There was a little water at the dip near Brice's place, but the water markers signalled it was super shallow. I carried on, thinking about Dan and hoping he was okay. Even though he'd sounded a little pissed off about his parents, his concern had radiated down the line. It was understandable, both his frustration and his worry.

Aware the location Dan told me was coming up, I slowed, already assuming that where they were, the road would be cut off.

In Alan's defence, I'd never known this patch of the road to be so deep you couldn't cross safely, and I expected he'd assumed the same thing.

I spotted their car in the distance, angled in a ditch, water covering its rear end and reaching the front bumper. Another vehicle was parked this side of the water, a couple of guys talking to who I assumed were Hazel and Alan. As I drew closer, I exhaled. It was definitely Dan's parents. They were safe.

I could only see the face of one of the men. I didn't recognise him. He was a little taller than Alan, probably a few years older than me, and sporting a beard that I was a little envious of even from a distance.

He said something to Alan, who laughed, then looked over at me, giving me a wave.

As soon as I pulled up, I hopped out. "You guys okay?"

Hazel took the few steps in my direction and hugged me, giving me a tight squeeze. "Thank you so much for coming to get us. I swear it's a good job; else I would have hitched a lift and left Alan here."

I hugged her back, pressing a kiss on her cheek. "Hey, Hazel. No worries. Lucky I headed out then. Who knows what trouble Al would get into else." I snorted good-naturedly. "Hey, Al."

Alan sent me an apologetic smile and shook my hand. "Thanks for coming, son. I've gotta say, I'm relieved you came and not Dan."

I laughed. "I'll bet. Best run for cover when he sees you, though. Not sure he's going to let you live this down for a while."

"Don't I know it." Alan then glanced in the direction of the blokes who he'd been talking to when I arrived. I followed his line of sight, my eyes widening a fraction when my gaze connected with Nick's.

"Nick?"

A slight pink spread across his cheeks, and he bobbed his head at me. "Ross. We came across Mr and Mrs Madison here, not realising this way was cut off. They said someone was on their way to collect them."

"Right, yeah," I said, pulling myself together from the surprise of seeing him here. A flick of my stare to his side landed on the man I didn't recognise. Before I could say anything else, a car door opening caught my attention.

"Daddy, can we go yet?"

A boy, no older than four or five hauled himself out of the Land Cruiser, and Nick turned, calling out, "Murphy, we said no getting out of the truck."

The man to Nick's side shook his head. "I'll get him. You know how bloody nosey that boy is." He stepped towards the car, and I couldn't look away if I tried, my brain misfiring at what I was seeing, trying to piece together their story.

A moment later, the guy returned, Murphy all but skipping while holding his hand.

"George, this is Ross, the school librarian." My eyes met Nick's when he spoke before travelling to George. "Ross, this is my husband, George, and this rascal here is our son, Murphy."

Well, blow me hard and colour me surprised.

The hours I'd spent defending myself from Nick

blurred in my spinning brain, right alongside the hours spent convincing myself I was brave and strong and wouldn't take any shit, right before I'd vomit, anxious about what the day would bring.

Rendered speechless, I nodded at George, unable to say a word.

Heat engulfed me, taking me unaware, and amusement bubbled in my chest.

No fucking way I'd release it, though, certain it would come out sounding hysterical. But, fuck, seriously? Not knowing what to do, I clamped onto the inside of my cheeks, the inappropriate laughter edging dangerously close.

I swallowed hard, unsure how to process this information or even begin to analyse my reaction.

This... development didn't impact me... my life one bit, so why the hell was my brain misfiring?

The sound of my name snapped my attention, dragging me away from my thoughts.

Worried eyes peered back at me, kind and so similar to her son's.

"Right." My smile was tight, controlled as I clapped my hands together. It was the only reaction I could manage while hysteria loomed. "Let's take a look at this car of yours and see what's going on."

George and Alan helped work out the best way to tow out the car, and we agreed—albeit reluctantly on my part—it made sense for George to do the towing. His Land Cruiser would handle the job much easier than my Hilux, so it wasn't even anything I could disagree with.

Hazel stayed close to Nick and Murphy, seemingly enjoying entertaining the young boy, while I moved on autopilot.

By the time we were ready to haul the car out of the ditch, I was more in control of my reaction and less robotic with my movements. It was best I didn't think about Nick's revelation. There'd be enough time for that afterwards.

"Okay," I called out through the open window of Alan's car. I'd volunteered to wade in and jump in behind the wheel to help steer the vehicle out.

George gave me the thumbs-up, and I braced, ready for the jolt. It came a moment later, Alan standing just off to the side, shouting the occasional instruction at George. I steered the best I could, wincing when I heard a loud, metallic scrape, but the noise didn't halt the car, not with the power of the V8 Land Cruiser.

"Got it!" Al shouted. I grinned despite the weird

tightness in my chest. "You beaut!" Al followed up with a tap on his SUV's bonnet.

Once George had stopped, I engaged the handbrake and exited the car, a slush of water coming out with me. I had no idea if the engine had survived the ordeal or not, but knowing Dan's parents, they'd have good insurance so they'd be covered.

"I'll just follow you," George said.

I bobbed my head. "Sounds good. It's not too far from here."

George offered a smile, and I couldn't help but think he seemed like a really decent guy, and in that case, how on earth had he ended up with the likes of Nick?

Within twenty minutes, we were at my house. I'd shot off a text to Dan before leaving, letting him know his parents were with me and safe. I chose not to share my latest discovery with him. It seemed too much like a big deal to share via text.

We'd all piled out of the cars, and I eyed the group speculatively. Good manners had me struggling to keep my mouth shut from offering them a drink or something. They'd gone out of their way to help Alan and Hazel.

Before I could offer, Nick entered my line of

sight, his boy swinging on his hand. Murphy was all but bouncing up and down on the spot. I smiled in amusement at him and cast a glance at Nick. "Bathroom?"

"If that's okay." His smile was the warmest it had been, less tentative and forced.

"No worries. I'll open up and show you the way."

I led the two of them to the house while Alan and George got to work releasing the SUV. Hazel was rummaging around in the soggy interior, the occasional grumble freeing from its confines. My lips twitched. I had little doubt she'd be giving her husband hell about this.

Once inside my home, I pointed in the direction of the main bathroom. "Second door on the right."

"Thanks." Nick smiled again and rushed his boy to the bathroom.

While they sorted themselves out, I filled up the kettle and turned it on to make tea, then quickly checked in the nicer spare room—the "green" room that my brother regularly grumbled about remained unpainted. He hadn't been exaggerating about the colour either. It was legit an eyesore, but it had become a bit of a joke over the years, and I was reluctant to paint it just to get a rise out of Craig.

The bed was made, sheets clean, and I turned on the air conditioning unit. I wasn't sure how long we'd have power for, but I'd make the most of it. While I was on a different grid than the south side of town, I did expect to lose power at some point.

The heavy thudding of feet had me turning to see Murphy racing along the hallway. He stopped before me in the kitchen.

"You all done?"

He bobbed his head. "Yep. My poop was big."

I chuckled loudly and flicked my attention to Nick when his mortified groan clued me in to him joining us.

"Sorry about Murphy. He likes to overshare."

"Big poops are sometimes worthy of conversation, aren't they, Murphy?"

His nod was big and overexaggerated. "I has nuthink in my tummy now," he said to me all wide-eyed and looking super cute. "Daddy, I's hungry."

"We'll be heading home soon, so you can get something then."

Murphy pouted, his bottom lip sticking out impressively.

"There's fruit in the bowl," I offered, my focus on Nick. "There's also crackers in the pantry."

Murphy eyed the bowl of fruit. "Can I have narna, Daddy?"

Nick's brows tugged together. "You sure that's okay?"

"Of course," I answered.

I could do this. The buffer of a kid made this so much more manageable.

"Thanks," he said and looked down at his son who peered up at him with all the innocence such a small child could. "You can get *one*," he emphasised. "And mind your manners."

Murphy bobbed up and down, looking far too excited at the prospect of eating a banana, but who was I to judge the kid? Swap that with a Magnum ice cream and I'd be bouncing around too.

His short legs ate up the distance from his dad to the fruit bowl. Once there, he hemmed and hawed, making a selection.

I chuckled and risked a glance at Nick. His focus was solely on his son, nothing but love and patience evident. When he flicked his attention to me, a warm smile remained on his lips, and probably for the first time ever, I saw the "handsome" in the guy previously shadowed by the ugly of his spite.

"How old's Murphy?" I asked, curiosity encouraging me to continue softening the animosity around us.

"Four next month."

And then my words dried up. I had nothing to follow up with. I was saved from the growing awkwardness by a triumphant "This one!" Murphy's smile was huge as he held it high in the air like a warrior sword. Then, without more prompting from his dad, he peered up at me. "Thank you for the narna."

"You're welcome. Shall we head back out and see what's going on?"

"'K." In a handful of strides, Murphy surprised the hell out of me when he reached my side and latched onto my hand.

Concerned, I shot Nick a look, but he watched on, offering a light shrug, and started heading out the door. Alrighty then, it seemed like I had a new mate.

"Do you need help peeling the banana?" I asked as we stepped back out into the sunshine.

"I try myself." He then plonked his arse down on the gravelly ground and tried his hardest to open the banana, with fairly decent success since none fell in the puddles of mud littering the space.

Seeking distance from Nick, I headed over to Alan, George, and Hazel. Once at the bonnet, I paused next to Alan. "How's it looking?" Car mechanics wasn't part of my general skillset. I could change the oil, and that was about it.

"George seems to think the car may not be totalled." Alan winced as he spoke and side-eyed his wife.

"*May* being the key word here. The water rose high, so it may have got into everything. If it has, I expect the insurance company will write it off. But I can check properly tomorrow, so at least you get a better idea of what to expect."

"That'd be great, thanks, George." Alan bobbed his head in appreciation.

Curious, I asked, "You know a lot about cars?"

He offered me a friendly smile. "Mechanic."

"In that case, I imagine you're going to be seriously busy over the coming weeks," I responded with a chuckle. A thought pulled me up short. "Can you get home?" Dread stirred in my gut that they lived on the other side of the creek.

"We're not too far away, over on Larkson Valley Road."

"That's a relief, especially with Murphy."

"Definitely. It's a lot easier now he's potty trained. That's a time I never want to live through again." Amusement creased his eyes.

So many questions burned in me about Nick and his happy little family, but I swallowed each and every one down, moving my attention to Alan. "Why don't I get you and Hazel settled in?"

"Sounds good. Thanks for putting us up."

"No worries. Hardly going to turn you away, am I?"

At my words, Hazel appeared at my side, her arm sliding around my waist where she squeezed lightly. "I think there's a lot to catch up with." Her face tilted up, and she beamed at me.

"How about you leave the third degree to Dan," I said with a polite chuckle. It didn't matter that I knew both of them super well; with Dan and me being together and this the first time seeing them since, this was weird.

"Please, that son of mine doesn't tell me anything. If I want to know the details, it's best I go to the source."

George shifted, closing the bonnet. When I glanced at him, I saw curiosity in his expression and wondered whether his husband had mentioned me at all. I had little doubt that Nick hadn't spared me a thought for years, though with his apparent unease since he started school, I imagined he would have shared at least something about our awkward reunion.

"Ross is dating our son, Dan," Hazel offered, I expected reading the unasked question in George's eyes.

"I didn't realise it was Dan Madison." Nick's voice appeared from behind me. I glanced over my shoulder to where he stood just a few metres away, his son by his side.

My brows dipped low. I pulled my lips into my mouth, not sure how to respond to that or even if I needed to.

That first time we'd seen each other in the library, I'd mentioned my boyfriend, Dan, in hearing distance, never mentioning his last name, and why would I?

"You guys were tight in high school." Pink spread up his neck when he spoke.

Hazel answered before I could. "All three of the boys were always together, and it's so wonderful that Dan and Ross are finally a couple." Her gushing was sweet, and she was utterly oblivious to Nick's discomfort.

His husband, however, not so much. George moved to Nick's side immediately, and I turned and saw him catch his husband's attention. While I couldn't see George's expression since his back was to us, Nick bobbed his head a moment later. It was a minute movement, but with my focus so intent, I didn't miss it.

George then held Nick's hand before turning his focus back to us. "We're going to head off, unless you need help with anything."

"We're all good, thanks. And thank you for helping and the tow," I offered, my relief renewed that they were leaving so I didn't have to engage in a conversation with Nick.

"No worries. I'll stop by in the morning."

"Thanks," Alan said, his arms filled with some of the items Hazel had removed from their car.

Just as they headed towards their vehicle, a loud bleat echoed, snagging my attention immediately. Remembering about Bessie, I jerked my head in the direction of the sound, only to groan when it clearly wasn't Bessie.

Benji stood on the veranda, right outside the spare room window. He bleated again, focus on us, mouth wide and making a damn racket.

"Goat, Daddy!" Murphy squealed in delight and made a run for it, managing only two small steps before Nick swooped him up.

"Not right now, Murphy."

But his boy was having none of it as he wriggled and pleaded with his dad.

Hating the sadness of his pleas, I offered, "I have to round him up and put him back in the paddock. It should only take a couple of minutes, so you're free to help."

Surprise popped Nick's eyes wide open when he looked at me.

"Yes. Can we help, Daddy?"

My smile was warm at Murphy's eagerness.

"Yeah, that'd be great, thanks." Gratitude filled Nick's features as he bobbed his head at me.

"Okay," I directed at Murphy. "No racing towards him, though, else he'll think you're playing a game."

Wide-eyed, the three-year-old looked at me. "He play games?"

I chuckled. "Only chase."

The boy all but vibrated with energy.

"Perhaps save the games till next time."

He bounced his agreement, and when I reached his side, he reached out and gripped my hand. Since it was okay the last time, I assumed that it would be again, but I side-eyed Nick just in case. While I had a whole history of issues with the man, there wasn't a chance I wanted to make the wrong move with his son.

His attention was on his son as Murphy chattered away about the goat, so we continued on, my smile forming quickly at the kid's enthusiasm.

"Now's the tricky part," I said, pausing a few metres from the steps that led to the front of the veranda. "We need to make sure he doesn't make a run for it."

Murphy listened intently, his gaze on mine.

"You know how we do that?" I asked.

"No." He shook his head.

"Benji here has a favourite treat. I think it may be one of yours too."

"Lollies?" His face split into a grin. Nick's laughter joined mine.

"Not lollies, but bananas."

"Narnas like me?"

"Yep. So if you guys want to wait here so Benji doesn't make a run for it, let me grab the banana, and we'll see just how much he likes them, okay?"

Once again, Murphy all but vibrated, this time a big head nod joining his bouncing.

I dashed inside and grabbed a banana, and quickly returned to Nick and Murphy. I opened the banana and broke off a small chunk, then showed him how to hold it properly so Benji could take it from him without his fingers being nibbled on.

It took barely any time at all for Benji to follow his nose and discover his favourite treat. Together, we led him back to the paddock, and I checked Bessie.

"Is she pregnant?" Nick's deep voice startled me, him having kept quiet during our goat herding.

"Yeah. Due any time now."

"She having baby?" Murphy scrunched his nose and peered over at Bessie, who munched on grass, her swollen stomach on show.

"Hopefully very soon. You'll have to ask your dad if you can come visit when it's born."

Immediately, Murphy swung around and latched onto Nick's legs, head angled back. "Can we, Daddy? He's said we could."

"Ross, not he," Nick clarified. At the correction, my heart raced, though with no real idea why that was. "If Ross says it's okay, then we'll definitely make it happen."

Murphy bounced up and down, still latched on to Nick, who immediately held him back. He sent me a wry grin. "Headbutts aren't fun."

Laughter spilled out of me, surprising the both of us if Nick's startled look was anything to go on. "I can imagine," I said, sobering a little.

"Come on, Murphy, we best get going." He reached out for his son's hand, and we turned and strolled towards his Land Cruiser. "Thanks for the goat offer," he said as we reached the back door.

"No worries. I can let you know when the kid arrives."

A smile lifted his lips, the gesture seeming a little easier. "Thanks."

Once they'd got Murphy strapped in, we said goodbye, and I stood next to Dan's parents as they pulled out.

"They seem like a nice family," Hazel said at my side.

"Yeah, they do." It was that knowledge and all I'd learned about Nick that I needed to navigate and get my head around. While I felt more at ease than when I'd first stumbled on Nick and his family, what I knew then compared to today's reality were at loggerheads.

And only I could unravel that mess.

I needed Dan home, safe and sound, so I could talk this out. Hopefully that would happen tomorrow.

"Come on, let's go inside and get things sorted." I made my way back to the house, carrying the bag

Hazel had been holding. Maybe then, I'd check on Bessie properly and have some time to myself to think this new development over.

It was probably the safest bet, especially as Hazel hadn't had the chance yet to grill me about my relationship with her son.

20
___

DAN

It had become a habit over the past couple of months to fall into my bed bone tired. Last night hadn't been any different.

Fighting nature was impossible. That had never been as clear as since returning to the Sunny Coast hinterland, not that the city didn't have its fair share of mayhem either. I only had to look back to the horrific floods sending raging waters through the streets of Brisbane a few years back to appreciate that.

The extremes here seemed more visceral, even though they made me feel so bloody lucky that our "extremes" were a damn sight less horrendous than other parts of our state or country at large.

It didn't mean I couldn't give myself five minutes to feel weary, though, and wish we could get a break.

Shutting off the alarm on my phone, I yawned and stretched wide. My hand brushing alongside the empty space beside me wasn't a sensation I wanted to get used to.

The good thing was, despite the full-on day of rescue yesterday and a couple of close calls, there'd been no fatalities. The water had also already been receding by the time I'd dragged myself home, barely managing a shower before faceplanting on my mattress.

But it was already time to get up and see what needed to be done, and I thanked Christ that last night we'd received extra support from further afield, so I was actually able to get some rest.

Having a quick shower to help wake up, I contemplated the likelihood of being able to get to Ross's this afternoon.

He'd gone above and beyond yesterday to help my parents. And while his support wasn't a surprise, it still made my heart race and dip like a roller coaster, reminding me of those words that had spilled out yesterday morning.

We'd spoken for barely a minute last night. My folks were safe, Ross sounded more tired than I anticipated, and Bessie was still pregnant. In our brief conversation, neither of us had mentioned the L word, nor did I let the words stumble unbidden again.

There was no doubt I'd say them again. The words were out there now, caught in the invisible connection between us. I did not want them to disappear. My tired overshare had just sped my declaration up a little. My stomach flipped at the thought—in both anticipation and nervous excitement.

I swilled off the suds, then dried off. I'd make a coffee this morning to-go rather than race out of here like fierce rapids were after me. I turned on the machine and flicked off a quick text to Ross while I waited.

Me: Just about to head back out. I'll let you know any updates as soon as I do. Stay safe.

Before long, I'd made my way to the station. A few of the guys arrived at the same time as me. I greeted them with a tired smile, and we walked in together, all hugging our coffees.

Craig was already there.

"Get much rest?" he asked when I leaned against the wall at his side. A quick look around told me the chief would lead briefing, but a few bodies were still missing.

"Not too bad, about six hours. Slept soundly, though. You?"

"About the same."

Movement off to the side brought my attention to the last couple of stragglers, and before I could say anything else, Frank called our attention and started laying out the plans for the day.

"With the water already receding, we're going to ensure nobody enters areas and houses still flood affected. The SES is leading the clean-up while we're focusing on clearing roads. This'll mean trees, debris, any vehicles. I shouldn't need to remind any of you not to be crossing flooded roads and only be tackling anything where it's safe to do so. If there's an emergency situation, the usual protocols are in place.

"Be extra vigilant for wildlife," he continued, and Craig shuddered at my side, hating snakes especially. I wasn't a fan myself, but I had a healthy respect for them—from a distance. "Just keep your heads on straight and wits about you. We're splitting into three crews."

I chugged back my coffee before checking and collecting equipment, then joined Craig, Sandra, and Lee. Sandra hauled herself into the driver seat, and we checked our comms. Sandra verified where we were heading first: Michelin Avenue, where there was a road blockage.

Out on the road, we drove slowly. While there weren't a lot of vehicles about, there were plenty of people out and about, most looking like they were ready for hard work supporting their neighbours who'd been impacted.

We managed to get to the outskirts of town to Michelin Avenue. It looked here that the homes weren't too severely impacted. Most were raised a good metre off the ground. While some flood water and debris remained, this part of town didn't appear to be badly off.

Water splashed and moved right alongside us, probably a couple of inches still on the ground, and up ahead, a couple of cars were stationary, both parked haphazardly. A small gum had uprooted from one of the gardens, smashing through a fence and stretching out on the road.

Sandra parked, and we got to work, first shifting the abandoned vehicles, both left unlocked, making the task refreshingly easy. Once the cars were out of the way, we suited up with our protective gear and chainsaws.

The aim was to clear the road so vehicles could

get through safely. The council guys would head over as soon as they could with their woodchippers to finish off the job. We weren't about keeping things tidy. Our goal was safe access.

We worked on the branches, since those were the main things blocking the road. The limbs took some work, but I was grateful we didn't need to mess with the trunk at large.

We zipped through the wood, the scent of gum heavy in the air with the fresh cuts. Between the four of us cutting and shifting the branches off the road, we made short work of the task. In a couple of hours, we were done and moving on to the next job we received from Sammy via comms.

On our way to our third road clearage, I checked my texts, finding a message from Ross. I grinned before even reading it.

"Let me guess, Ross?" Craig said from my side.

"He thinks Bessie's finally in labour."

"Him and that bloody goat." He chuckled.

I smirked in agreement. The goats were pains, but I understood why Ross put up with them. They were entertaining and I supposed a little cute. "Mum will be loving it."

"I'll bet. I wouldn't be surprised if she tries to steal the kid away."

"You know it." Mum was such a big softie with animals. It had only been since their travelling days they hadn't been surrounded by animals of some description. It made for fun, exciting times growing up, never knowing what Mum adopted or nursed back to life. Each day offered a possible adventure.

"You remember when she thought rescuing those couple of bunnies would be a good idea?"

I shook my head in memory as I typed out a quick message to Ross. "Yeah. The multitude of new bunnies created as a result and then the hefty fine she received afterwards."

Dad had been pissed off, especially as he'd reminded Mum countless times that keeping rabbits as pets in Queensland was illegal.

"Where we off to next?" I asked Sandra, having not really paid attention to the details of the next job.

"Heading over to Michaels Creek over at Hawthorn. There's cattle on the road there."

"Alive?" My brows dipped into a frown, hating the idea of the alternative.

"Yeah. The owner's on the scene. Needs a hand."

That was a relief. I texted the details to Ross, who'd asked where I was heading to.

Ross: Be safe.

Me: Good luck with Bessie.

As we drove closer to our next stop, I couldn't help but wonder how many more call-outs we'd need to take. My thoughts briefly went to the day after tomorrow being Australia Day, aware that in many ways, our community would be "celebrating" the best way possible, especially considering the actual date was shadowed with so much unease considering the significance of the date to Indigenous Australians. Tomorrow, for our community, we'd be spending it supporting our town, its occupants, and stepping up to make sure everyone was safe.

Everyone mucking in together seemed significant somehow, and despite being tired, despite wishing the day would be over already and still waiting to see if it was safe to travel to Ross's, I was where I should be.

"Bloody hell."

Craig's exclamation startled me and drew my attention to the scene ahead. My brows shot high, and Sandra's "Fuck" had me nodding in absolute agreement.

Once parked, we clambered out of the truck, our eyes taking in the mayhem before us.

Ankle-deep water spilled over the road, the usually shallow creek a good three feet high based on the multitude of cows converging in and around the area. The kicker was, at least seven of the cows weren't simply splashing around having a good time.

The bellowing was loud. I winced at the noise and the scene, knowing we were going to get wet and muddy. Looking closer at the creek, I counted the seconds it took a small twig to travel from one point to another about five metres away.

The muddy water wasn't travelling too fast, which offered some relief.

But it looked like those mud-splattered cows mooing their damn heads off were stuck good and tight. Meanwhile, the bloke on the other side of the creek was alone and trying his hardest to push those cows not trapped away and towards an open gate about twenty metres or so away. Part of the fence was down, creating a gaping hole where I expected the cows would happily become escape artists again given a chance.

"Let me head on over and see what's what."

We nodded at Sandra, Lee joining her to cross the flooded road while Craig and I watched on.

"I don't suppose we have waders in the truck?"

I snorted and shook my head at Craig.

He sighed. "Figures."

Despite the noisy cows and the distressed

bellowing that tugged at my gut, I took in the surroundings. We were only about fifteen minutes out from Ross's place, and the vista here was almost as spectacular as the view from his house.

Even with the muddy creek, it was easy to look beyond that to the rolling fields leading to the large valley. With the water still resting on the ground of oats and grass that struggled to soak it all up, it appeared like a sparkling blanket, glistening in the mid-afternoon sun.

Give it a week, and this area would be flourishing with fresh shoots and regrowth. It was the only positive outcome I could think of post-flood—all the much-needed water saturating the earth.

The chaos and damage was a hefty price to pay for the water, though.

Movement on the road caught my attention. Sandra and Lee headed towards us. Their expressions told me that none of us would be coming out of this job clean or dry.

"Old mate Bill over there has someone heading over now with some wire to do a quick fix of the fence. He's been trying to keep them close together and stop them from panicking, but those ones stuck are making that impossible.

"The plan is to shift those free, get them through

the gate. Bill's going to park his Cruiser in front of the fence to try to deter them, then we need to get these cows out."

"We're assuming it's just mud that's got them trapped. Just unfortunate, I guess, but we'll need ropes and get in to see what we can do," Lee added.

"Got it," Craig said, and I bobbed my head.

Together, we gathered the ropes, took a deep breath, and focussed on getting in and out as quickly as possible.

Quick no longer seemed to be the word of the day, however.

Sorting the loose cows had been surprisingly straightforwards, all of us walking that fine line between shocked and relieved when we ushered in the fifty or so cows.

The ones trapped weren't being as hospitable.

Between the flies buzzing around our faces, the mozzies at our ears, and the tired cows, Craig slipping in the water seemed like the icing on the cake. All of us found it more hilarious than we should have. Hysteria wasn't surprising, with tiredness biting at our heels.

"You all right?" I gave him a hand and tugged him up, wishing it would have been so easy with the cows.

"Fuck," he grumbled. "Yeah." A wry grin formed on his lips and my mouth twitched. "There's so many rocks underfoot. Those bastards are slippery."

They'd tripped us all up too. A bunch scattered the embankment as well as underfoot, making our movement more precarious. Two of the cows we'd released had managed to get trapped by rocks. Another two had simply been sucked in by the mud. We still had three more to go, but fortunately, another couple of the farmer's friends had arrived to give a helping hand.

"You need to hold my hand?" My smile was wide as I wagged my eyebrows at him.

"Piss off," he muttered and shoved me a little.

I chuckled and took a tentative step forwards, wishing like hell I could see where my foot landed. Craig stepped with me, the both of us moving slowly towards our next target. His "Shit" was the warning I needed to grab hold of him as he stumbled.

"You been knocking back shots or something without telling me?"

He rolled his eyes. "Don't I wish."

"My hand's sounding more appealing right now, huh?" I teased, still gripping his forearm.

He opened his mouth to speak but was cut off by a loud cuss. The two of us jerked our attention towards the shout. The cow we were heading towards bellowed and thrashed.

Surprising the shit out of me, she actually moved, getting herself free. The cheer on my lips was cut off abruptly by another loud cuss, followed by "Snake. King brown."

With the cow taking panicked strides in our direction and the threat of a snake that I assumed was heading this way too, an errant "Oh fuck" spilled from me as I clung on to Craig and lurched to the closest bank.

Craig's weight slammed into me, shoving me down, the two of us falling. I registered a mouthful of mud and water before pain ricocheted across my forehead, and the world went fuzzy and then black.

21

ROSS

The mid-afternoon sun beat down on us, unrelenting and right on temperature for this time of year. Alan was helping me muck out the goat stall, preparing it for Bessie, who was unusually quiet. Benji, meanwhile, kept his distance, nudging against Valkyrie and annoying her rather than us, which was something.

"Does she look to be straining to you?" Alan leaned against his fork, eyeing Bessie. I followed his line of sight, focussing on her stomach.

A thrill of anticipation buzzed in my chest. "I think you're right."

While we'd been clearing up, she'd remained quiet, content to let us clean up around her. I'd hoped it meant she was close, getting ready to give birth. Finally it looked like the wait was over.

The sound of a car engine dragged our attention out of the goat stall. It was George. This morning, he'd stopped by briefly to say he couldn't look at Alan's car till this afternoon instead. Talk about timing.

"I'll go see to George, and I'll let Hazel know about the goat." He left with a wave while I focussed on gathering the towels and nose sucker.

Not knowing how many kids she'd be having may mean Bessie would need a helping hand, so I was prepared as I could be. After watching a couple of videos, I already felt reassured that if I had to assist, it'd be a lot easier than the time I had to help Valkyrie, whose calf had got wedged.

Gravel crunching under feet headed my way, and I looked up, startling a little when I saw Nick. This time it didn't take long for me to dislodge the air clamped in my throat at seeing him. Partly because my attention dropped on to his young son, who did a small hop and skip as he held his dad's hand; the other reason was that yesterday's impromptu meeting had settled some of the unease in my gut.

Plus, there was no abrupt laughter, so I called it progress.

Knowing there wasn't going to be any vileness sent my way for being gay had soothed any lingering doubts I'd had. But also, he'd stepped up by helping Alan and Hazel, and more than that, he'd trusted me with his son.

Last night before heading to sleep, I'd spared barely more than a thought on the man and his family, examined my reaction. In many ways, I didn't bother psychoanalysing myself or my response since seeing Nick again or since discovering he was married to a man.

There was no point in as much as I didn't need my thoughts swirling in my mind, tugging at any lingering insecurities I may have had.

Life was too bloody short for that.

Instead, I considered what, if anything, I was going to do next. The jury was still out, because I didn't know if I wanted to drag up the past with him.

I certainly didn't want to hash anything out. I'd be full of shit, though, if I didn't admit that an acknowledgement that how he'd treated me had been all kinds of fucked up wouldn't go amiss. Potentially it'd be cathartic, even.

But for now, with the man and his boy heading my way, I could be myself. I could smile at his cute kid, and I could return friendly conversation.

"Hey, Ross."

"G'day, Nick. Murphy." I encouraged them to enter the stall and get out of the fierce rays.

"Alan said you might be having a new goat."

"I think so. There's been a couple of contractions I noticed while getting some things ready, so hopefully she's ready to push soon."

"She have babies out her bum?" Wide-eyed, Murphy stared at Bessie, fascination evident in every angle on his young face.

I pressed my lips together and looked up at Nick. A wide grin was directed my way, drawing a chuckle from me.

"Not quite," he said. "Just a little lower than her bum, I think."

Murphy nodded and angled his head, scrunching his nose as if to get a good look.

"I don't know how long it'll take, but you guys can stay and watch, maybe help out." The offer came with surprising ease.

Nick's brows all but met his hairline at my offer. "Oh wow, yeah." He cleared his throat and peered down at his son. "How about it, Murphy? You want to stay and watch baby goats being born?"

"Yes!" He jumped up and down.

"Hush." Nick knelt beside him. "We can only

stay if you're not shouting and jumping around, okay? I think…" His gaze lifted to mine. "What's her name?"

"Bessie."

"Right, so, Bessie here," he continued, refocusing on Murphy, "has a lot of hard work to do. It's not going to be easy to get her kid out of her."

Murphy stilled immediately and plonked himself down on his backside in the fresh hay. "Is that what Laney did?"

Before Nick could answer, Bessie shifted, drawing my attention to her. The goat's stomach was contracting, her whole body moving with the effort.

Surprisingly, she was quiet, another sure sign that it was finally time. Picking up the towel and suction nozzle, I shifted closer and knelt in the hay, relieved Alan and I had time to clean up properly.

Bessie's attention was on me for a moment before she looked away and strained. Low murmurs were coming from Nick, and I caught enough to hear he was explaining what was happening.

"Ooh, I'm just in time," Hazel said softly, entering the space but keeping her distance.

"Yeah. Looks like the kid's breeching."

"Is it just the one?" she asked.

I shrugged. "Not sure."

We sat back and watched quietly until a tiny black baby goat came into the world a few moments later. I edged closer, towel in hand, and cleaned its face, going for the mouth and nostrils when Bessie seemed content to let me take over.

Once I was sure the airways were clear of gunk, I waited a beat, excitement unfurling in my stomach when the baby lifted its head and opened its mouth.

With Bessie still making no effort to encourage the newborn over, I rubbed the kid down a little, then backed off, watching as it already made an attempt to stand. This got Bessie's attention, and she sniffed at it, giving a firm lick, encouraging the gorgeous black bundle of cuteness closer to her head.

Bessie cleaned her baby off for a few minutes, and I glanced over at Nick and Murphy. Nick wore a soft smile while Murphy's nose was scrunched.

"You okay, Murphy?"

"It was all yucky."

A chuckle escaped the three of us.

"Yeah, it was, but look at what a good job Bessie's doing at cleaning it." I smiled wide.

"I think she's contracting again," Nick said, and I whipped my head around to see he was right.

"Daddy, was I licked clean?"

I held back my burst of laughter, not wanting to startle Bessie.

"Uhm, that'd be a big no, Murphy. You were cleaned in a bath." Amusement laced Nick's reply, and I grinned, casting them a quick glance and wondering at how peculiar this thing called life could be.

It took twenty minutes for Bessie to be the proud mum of three kids, a boy and two girls. She was chilled enough to allow us all to have a little pet too.

We were heading to the house to wash up when Alan approached. "Everything all good?"

"Yeah, three new goats to cause chaos and mayhem," I answered.

"Sounds like you have at least two decent names there," Nick said at my side.

I snickered and glanced over at him. "If they're anything like their parents, then they're highly suit-able, for sure."

"You mind if I borrow your car to take a look at how the creek's doing heading to my place?" Alan wiped his oily hands on a rag as he spoke.

"Sure, as long as there's no plans for a mad dash across any flooded roads." My brow quirked high at Alan.

"To be sure, I'll go with you," Hazel said, stepping towards her husband. "Make sure you don't wreck another car."

"George here thinks it might be salvageable," Alan grumbled, glancing back at the man whose head was under the bonnet of the waterlogged car.

Hazel didn't seem convinced, however, and honestly, neither was I. Not with the mini waterfall that had followed me out of the driver door when I'd exited yesterday.

Once I'd given them my keys and Hazel promised me they wouldn't use my ute as a kayak, they left, leaving me alone with some of the newest additions to the town.

"If we head to the house, I'll grab you a clean towel so you guys can wash up."

Nick bobbed his head and took hold of Murphy, who'd been sat at his other dad's feet, picking up the few tools scattered on the ground. "Sounds good."

"You need a cold drink, George?"

"Yeah, that'd be great, thanks, Ross," he said, peeking out from behind the bonnet to answer.

"Give me five."

"No worries."

We headed up, and I set up Nick and Murphy in the guest bathroom while I went to my small en suite. Drying off my hands, I paused when I heard my phone ring. I dashed over to the chest of drawers where I'd left it, not wanting it to flip over to my voice mail in case it was Dan.

"Craig, hey," I answered.

When there was no response, I frowned and looked at the screen, wondering if he'd butt dialled me. It wouldn't be the first time. We were still connected.

I called louder, "Craig, you there?"

All at once, I was blasted with sound and a punch of dread.

"Shit. I'd hit mute," Craig said. His voice sounded off, or maybe it was the indistinguishable loud noises in the background making me think that.

"You okay?"

"Yeah, fine," he rushed to say. "Dan's hurt. He's just being taken to the hospital now."

The punch of dread was nothing compared to the cold hit of fear sliding over my skin and sinking into my veins.

"I'm coming." I didn't recognise the icy calm of my voice. It was at complete odds with the heavy pounding of my heart or the rush of chaos churning my gut.

"Just hold your damn horses a second."

I paused as he spoke to me, running through

everything that happened, and explaining to me the situation. I heard it all, but not a single word sank in, my brain simply latching on the fact that Dan was hurt and I needed to be with him.

"Just let me keep you updated."

"Nope."

Craig sighed, the sound weary. "Listen, I'm not even sure if the roads are clear."

"I said I'm coming. I'll find a way to get through." My tone offered no room for negotiation. I'd walk through any high water if I had to. "I won't be long."

I ended the call, more than aware I'd asked no clarifying questions. It didn't matter what had happened, and the last thing I wanted to know was whether it was serious.

All I could think of was getting to Dan. Craig and Dan would be pissed off at me for sure, but fuck if I could even give a shit about that right now.

I just needed to get to the hospital.

The sound of the closing bathroom door jolted me into action.

I tugged on a clean shirt and bounded out the room, all but running into Nick and Murphy.

Wide-eyed, Nick stopped in his tracks, taking in my appearance. "What's wrong?"

"I have to get to the hospital." As soon as the

words were out there, I remembered Alan had my car. *Fuck.*

"I'll take you," Nick said immediately.

There was no hesitation, no questions, just a simple recognition of the desperation that poured off me.

I hesitated, thinking about Murphy and recalling Craig's words about the roads possibly not being clear. "The roads...." I grimaced and looked at his boy before returning my focus to Nick.

"I'll get you there. Murphy can stay with his daddy."

It seemed as though that was all he had to say on the matter. He bobbed his head and led Murphy out of the house. The action got my brain working, helping to clear some of the noise buzzing in my mind.

I swiped up my wallet, still clutching my phone in my hand.

By the time I had my boots back on and was outside, George was nodding at whatever his husband was saying to him, his eyes serious and holding warning. A chaste kiss followed before Nick glanced at me and indicated towards his Cruiser.

"What shall I tell Alan and Hazel?" George said, stopping me in my tracks.

Fuck, I hadn't even thought of them. I pushed aside the sliver of guilt and hollered, "I'll call them now, see where they're at. If I can't get in touch, let them know I'll give them an update as soon as possible and will tell them if the roads are clear." I paused outside the passenger door. "Help yourself to whatever you need, and thank you, seriously."

"No worries. Keep each other safe."

I swallowed hard at George's words, feeling his worry like a fresh wave of heaviness. I resolved there and then that I wouldn't put his husband at risk.

While I needed to get to the hospital, I wouldn't be the reason to potentially put someone else there in the process.

After a brief nod, I jumped in the Land Cruiser, eyeing the snorkel and hoping that if there was any water, that it would be slow-moving enough for us to not even have to hesitate to get through.

We rode in silence as I called Hazel. By the fourth attempt, I gave up, assuming her phone was either on silent or she'd left it at my house.

"You can't make this shit up," I said into the quiet car, my attention ahead, watching the distance for any signs of water.

"What's that?"

"This." I gestured with my hands to the world at

large. "Non-stop since December. It's like some sort of disaster movie, but with maybe a C-list cast, making it even more unbelievable." A humourless snort escaped me as I considered the shitshow. "And to think you've just moved back. Hell, maybe you should make a quick escape for it."

Nick made a quiet sound of not quite agreement but perhaps sympathetic amusement. "If we moved back before the fires, I'd probably think it was a sign for sure."

I glanced at him, latching onto the distraction his conversation offered. "So knowing about the fires didn't put you off?"

He didn't answer straight away. Instead, he gnawed at his bottom lip before releasing it and saying, "We sort of figured that the way the weather patterns and the whole bollocks of global warming is going, it could happen anywhere." I understood that thought process completely. "Dad died last year, so we decided it was a good time to move back, spend time with Mum. Let her be a grandma."

There was no sadness evident in his tone, just a matter-of-fact explanation.

"I didn't hear about your dad," I said. While we were a small town in the grand scheme of things, there were several thousand inhabitants in our catchment. I'd never known his dad. I didn't even know his name. "Sorry to hear about your loss."

Nick pursed his lips and expelled a heavy breath. A flicker of guilt sparked to life in my chest that our conversation had brought him down. "Thanks, but don't be. He was a bastard."

Bitterness laced his words, taking me by surprise.

Not knowing what to say, I kept quiet.

"Anyway," he continued after a beat, "we're back and finding our feet."

"How do you like the new job?" A chuckle escaped when I realised how pointless my question was, since the kids hadn't had the chance to start the new school year yet. "Well, the department?"

His mouth lifted into a small smile. "Everyone seems great. Welcoming." He cleared his throat. "Even you."

And there it was, the opening to the topic I wasn't sure I wanted to bring back to life, despite my curiosity. Aiming to deflect, I gave a light laugh. "That first meeting I give, cutting it short by a good hour is definitely a winner."

Glancing away, I let my stare unfocus on the scenery zipping by, acutely aware that we were nearing the creek that could possibly leave us unstuck and me wading on through and hoping like hell the water's current didn't take a liking to me.

The green blurred with the vibrant blue sky, the occasional brown trunk breaking the pattern.

Nick's words jolted my attention, the colours and world outside coming into sharp view. "I don't know why you haven't called me out or treated me the way I perhaps deserve, but I want to say I'm sorry. For it all."

For it all. The words bounced around my brain, a silent list forming of what exactly that had entailed. Reciting it aloud may perhaps give me a vitriolic five minutes, but then what?

"You were so fucking brave when we were kids. I envied you and your family so much. They had your back, supported you...." I glanced over to see him shaking his head, perhaps at himself. "Dad found something I should have kept well hidden when I was fifteen." Bitterness seeped into his tone.

I winced, imagining just what that was. There was no need to imagine either. The same thing had happened to me. The difference was our stories were so different.

When Mum had found some pretty dodgy magazines of mine, she'd put them back away with a pamphlet about safe sex and a packet of condoms.

Sure, I'd been humiliated as hell, my seventeen-year-old self unable to cope with a spotlight on me and wanking. But by then, I already had the support of my family.

It didn't take much imagination at all to deduce Nick's story was a world apart from my own.

"I was so envious of you," he said, and I still remained quiet. "And through it all, the whole damn time, I hated myself even more for what I was putting you through, encouraging my mates. And honestly, it still plays on my mind so fucking often."

I found my voice, words spilling out before they'd fully formed, but I embraced every syllable, his apology, whether for the distraction I needed so I didn't vomit from my concern for Dan or simply from the fact they were words perhaps I needed to hear.

Deep down, it didn't matter the reason. "So you moving back and realising I worked at the same school...." I left the words hanging.

Nick's snort held a little more amusement this time. "Gotta admit it felt like karma had finally started making her rounds."

I chuckled, the strange turn of events momentarily shadowing my upset. "I bet."

When he started slowing, my brows dipped low

as I glanced at him. He signalled ahead with a small chin lift, and I followed his line of sight. We'd hit the creek that had most definitely flooded the road.

"Shit."

"Come on." His voice was strong, resolved. "Let's go check it out and see what our next move is."

I appreciated the calm determination leveling his voice. Before I stepped out, Nick saying my name stopped me.

"I am sorry for what I did, how I treated you. And I'm sure as shit sorry if me being back here has hurt you." Sincerity bled into his features.

"Confused me more than hurt," I said, wanting to respond and finally move on, despite the need biting at my heels to get through the water already and to Dan. "And I believe you're sorry."

We got out of the car and raced to the water, checking for the flow since it was higher than the one-metre marker.

"If you can get me through this, I may just forgive you sooner rather than later." I shot him a grin, my nerves going crazy, my heart bouncing around like it was on a damn trampoline.

"Even if you don't, we've got this." He gave a firm nod, his gaze shifting to me. "Let's get you to the hospital."

There wasn't a chance I'd argue. If he was confident he could get through safely, I'd trust him to do so.

We jogged to the Cruiser, and he pressed a button or two before he drove towards the slow-moving water. The splash of tyres in the floodwater competed with the noise of the engine.

"Shit, it's deep."

"We've got this."

We continued through, the water probably halfway up the door. Water oozed out of the seals, quickly forming puddles at our feet.

"Shit, is this your or George's car?"

A burst of laughter broke free from Nick, tearing free my own. "George's. But he'll be fine. Just pissed he couldn't get to test this out himself."

We edged past the deepest point, the water nowhere near as high as I'd expected, and finally, we were out. "Holy crap, you did it. Thank you."

His eyes were alight with victory as he looked at me. "Let's get you to the hospital."

I nodded and immediately sobered, the distraction and the burst of adrenalin fading away. "I'll text Hazel and let her know the road's not yet safe to cross without a snorkel."

"That's probably a good idea." He didn't need to

clarify why, considering all that had happened yesterday. I shook my head as I typed out a message, struggling to believe it was only yesterday when Alan had bogged his car.

Just over twenty-four hours since Dan had told me he loved me without a second thought and without either of us discussing it since.

I should have said it back. Spilled those three words into our next conversation. They should have been the first words out of my mouth.

If something happened, I—

"We're here."

The interruption cut through my thoughts in an instant.

"I'll drop you outside the doors, then go and find somewhere to park. I can wait there—"

"No, come in. It's fine. Thanks. You got me here." I cast him the briefest of looks, my main focus on the nearing kerb.

"No worries. I'll be back as soon as possible."

I nodded, and as he pulled up, I leapt out of the Cruiser, barely waiting for him to fully stop. Then I was running the few metres towards the automatic doors.

Immediately my attention landed on Craig, who was pacing in the small space.

"You're here." Air whooshed out of him before his brows dipped low. "Thank God you're safe. How—"

I waved him aside. "Later. Where is he? What's happening?" Finally, my questions had arrived. "Can I see him?"

"Yeah, sure. I've been coming out every few minutes waiting for you. Come on." He waved at the receptionist, who buzzed us through. I followed close at his heels while Craig started telling me what happened.

When he mentioned a snake, my knees wobbled, and I was all but sure they'd have buckled if his next words of "wasn't bitten" hadn't registered.

"The doc's concerned, as he's slipped into unconsciousness twice since being admitted. Not for long, but enough they want an MRI."

I nodded, my heart stuttering. He was alive, breathing, and mostly awake. That was good, all so fucking good. But it wasn't all great.

"He's in here."

He let me step ahead of him into the small examination room.

As soon as my gaze landed on the stitches lining Dan's temple, I swallowed hard. I would not let my emotions bubble over. Not yet. Not here. Dan's eyes were closed, bruising already formed across his cheekbone, and he looked sickly pale.

Unable to stop myself, I zeroed in on his chest and the few wires hooked up there, watching the gentle motion as he breathed in and out, and I sagged a little—or perhaps a lot, since Craig's arm appeared around my waist.

"Why not go sit next to him?" he whispered. "I think he'll be taken for the MRI in just a few minutes."

I nodded and pulled myself together as I robotically put one foot in front of another, not taking my eyes off the man who owned a piece of my heart. It didn't matter if he didn't know it yet. He would.

As I sat on the plastic chair, it scraped across the floor. My wince morphed into a smile when Dan opened his eyes.

"Hey, you." His voice was gruff.

"You missed me, huh? Couldn't wait till tonight?"

His attempt to laugh stopped abruptly with a groan and furrowing of his brows. "Fuck, my head hurts."

"Smashing it on a rock will do that to a skull." My hand found his and I squeezed, and unable to wait another moment, I edged up and pressed my lips lightly to his. I pulled away, just enough to see his face in focus. "You had me worried, but you're going to be fine."

Pain etched into every inch of his face, all but his eyes that shot me his warmth. "I am, and you're here."

"I wouldn't be anywhere else, but let's not make a habit of coming into town for hospital visits." My lips touched his again, and I reluctantly eased back, taking a seat while still holding his hand.

"The roads, are they clear?"

"Not really," I admitted, maintaining my whisper. "But I've decided we need to get a Land Cruiser... with a snorkel."

Dan appeared startled, his eyes widening a fraction before once again he winced.

"Shit, sorry. How about we just sit quietly for a while, and we'll talk about this later? Craig said—"

The door opening cut me off. An orderly entered with a friendly smile.

"I need Dan so we can take a trip."

"He's all yours. Well, for just a little while, as long as you promise to bring him back," I said, standing, trying my hardest to appear relaxed. It was so much easier to pretend and not dive in deep to the panic swirling at the edges of my consciousness.

The man smiled. "How about you take a walk with us? He won't be long, and you can wait outside. That way, you know we won't be running off anywhere."

While we were joking around, my neediness was alive and well and desperate to not be far away from Dan.

"Sounds good, thanks." I squeezed Dan's hand before releasing him to allow the orderly to do his job. Quiet at the doorway, Craig looked on. "Hey, Craig." I stepped towards him and lowered my voice. "Nick brought me in. He's probably in the waiting room by now," I said, ignoring how wide his eyes opened. "Will you go check in on him?"

His stare bounced around my face before fixating on mine. "Uh, yeah, sure. But let me know if there's any news, yeah?"

"Of course." I grimaced, remembering once again I'd forgotten about Dan's parents. "Do you have Hazel or Al's number?" When Craig nodded, I continued. "You mind seeing if they pick up and give them an update, but make sure to remind them that the road's still flooded and not to attempt to come into town."

The questions were evident in his eyes, but he didn't bombard me. Instead, he said, "Yeah, of course." He then surprised the crap out of me and tugged me into his arms, giving me a tight hug. "He'll be okay." His words were just for me.

I nodded. "I know." I had to believe them, and saying them aloud threw them out wide into the universe. When I eased away, I took in just how wrecked Craig was and could only imagine his worry on top of how exhausted he was. "You okay?" We stepped to the side as the orderly started moving the bed Dan lay in. Eagerness to be at his side niggled at me, but Craig deserved my focus.

Craig's shrug startled me and a zip of concern hit me. I knew my brother almost as well as I knew myself. Him not batting me away with an "of course" meant he wasn't holding up.

My need to support him and desperation to be at Dan's side all but pulled me in two. The orderly pushed past us and glanced back at me. I gave him a nod, which Craig immediately caught.

"I'll be fine. Go with Dan. He needs you right now."

I floundered and reached out, clamping my hand on his forearm. "Would you prefer to come with me so we can talk?"

"Nope." He shook his head and glanced away. "Go on. I'll find Nick and find out exactly what you've been up to." While he attempted to tease, the tension latched on to his words. Craig was a stubborn arse, though, and there'd be no swaying him on this.

"Okay. I'll let you know as soon as we're back, and please sit down, grab a coffee or something before you fall down, yeah?"

He nodded, already backing away and heading towards the doors to the waiting room.

I raced over to the orderly. "Sorry, and thanks for waiting."

"No worries. Town's crazy at the moment. People are going through a lot." Understanding reflected in his voice as he started pushing the bed.

I moved a couple of steps forwards so I could see Dan. "You okay there, Dan?"

"Uh-huh," he mumbled, his eyes closed. "Better when my head stops trying to split in two."

I stroked his arm as we walked, promising myself to never take Dan or the ability to touch him, talk to him, for granted. A thick swallow caught in my throat, but I shoved it down into the depths.

"Do these doors open automatically?" I glanced over at the orderly.

"If you press that green button there, they will."

I did so, the double doors slowly opening.

"Just around this corner, we're stopping at the room on the right," he explained.

"Okay, thanks."

In a few strides we were there, and I gave one last gentle squeeze of Dan's arm before he was ushered away. A moment later, the orderly returned.

"It shouldn't take long. I'll be back in a few so I can take him back to the ER."

"Thanks."

And then he was gone, and I was blissfully alone in the corridor.

My back thumped against the stark-white wall, and I scooted down it till my backside met the floor. Tension worked its way along my body, seeming to touch every limb, every nerve ending on its journey.

My head fell forwards between my bent knees, and I focussed on breathing.

Between the rush of adrenalin travelling through the floodwater, the mindfuck of memories and emotions Nick had dragged to the surface, and my absolute fear for the man I loved, I was drained. Spent.

And then there was Craig.

A new wave of worry seeped into me.

Perhaps he'd just hit his wall. I expected everyone in the emergency services, regardless of role or position, was running on fumes. Yet here I was, wallowing in my own misfortune and anxiety.

I fought my reprimand aside, more than aware it was pointless and didn't serve any purpose.

I reminded myself again to breathe, right along me telling myself it was okay to react and have emotions.

Closing my eyes, I inhaled steadily before exhaling on five, needing to recentre myself. It meant I could then step up and make sure I was there for Dan, and of course, my brother too.

"We doing all right here?"

The voice took me by surprise. I jerked my head up to see the still smiling orderly.

"Yeah. Is he done?"

For a few beats, his focus remained on me before he glanced away, his attention moving to a set of lights I hadn't noticed. "Looks like it. I'll just double-check."

I stayed sitting on the floor, not ready to move until I knew Dan was ready. The double doors opening had me quickly standing, however.

On the bed, still and pale, Dan was only a shadow of the man I'd spent Sunday with. My heart stuttered in concern. While I knew concussions could be serious and knocked people about, I was sure they were super common and didn't usually require MRIs. Nor did they make people look like they were anaemic.

Or perhaps I didn't know shit and was reading too much into everything.

After dotting a gentle kiss on Dan's forehead, I returned to the room and simply waited, and waited some more.

Dan slept, with someone checking on him every now and then. The whole time I barely dragged my attention away from his sleeping form.

The sound of his heartbeat became my companion. There were no flashing alarms, no shrill bells, just strong and steady, like how it sounded when I pressed my ear against his chest.

Craig popped in once, bringing me a coffee, before retreating to Nick, but other than that, we remained alone. Me with my thoughts and Dan's reassuring heartbeat.

22

———

DAN

Everything hurt. Between the pounding of my head, my throbbing temple, the scratching at my eyes that felt like piercing shards of glass, all I wanted to do was sleep.

And I did, except for when what seemed every five minutes I was prodded, vitals checked, all surrounded by enough noise that I was sure I was going to hurl.

Through it all, Ross remained at my side, vigilant, speaking softly, and offering a familiar press of his skin against mine.

I recalled all that had happened, was even mildly aware of being admitted and moved to a private room. I was grateful as fuck, knowing there wasn't a chance I could cope with the added noise from other patients.

With no clue what time it was but sure it was something o'clock in the morning from the growing light seeping between the slats of the closed blinds, I risked a peek.

It took a couple of times to force my eyes open properly, exhaustion feeling like super glue against my lids.

Ross slept in a chair that looked sort of comfy, well, at least more than I expected in a hospital. His face was pale, drawn. Soft whiskers decorated his cheeks from a couple of days of not shaving.

I blinked a few times, marvelling that he was here, had managed to get to my side, not really comprehending how he'd made that happen. That thought was followed swiftly by a flash of pain in my head, causing me to wince. I bit back my groan, but not fast enough, apparently, since Ross jerked awake. His eyes flashed open, focus immediately on me.

"You're awake. You need a drink?" Despite his voice being thick with sleep, the sound still pressed against me like a healing balm.

"Yeah." I licked at my lips, not having realised just how thirsty I was. "Please."

A soft smile was shot my way, and even though I

had no idea why, I accepted it eagerly, storing it away with the thousands of different smiles I'd earned.

With surprising efficiency since he'd just woken, Ross got busy pouring me a cup of water, placing a paper straw in for good measure. "The nurse said to take your time and sip." He pressed a button on my bed. "I'm just going to raise this so you don't struggle, okay?"

I hummed in understanding, simply wanting the refreshing drink the water offered. By the time the bed was more upright, I was about to pounce on the liquid, my mouth feeling Sahara-dry. With a gentle pull, the slightly tepid water filled my mouth, and I didn't give a shit that I'd usually scrunch my nose and complain. Instead, I savoured every drop, appreciating the relief it offered.

Easing back after taking a couple of sucks, I sighed and closed my eyes.

"I'll organise you to have some more painkillers."

I blinked my eyes open. Ross stood at the end of the bed, concern etching deep lines between his brows.

"As long as they don't make me sleepy."

When he pursed his lips as though to argue, I couldn't resist smirking.

His gaze narrowed at me.

"What?' I asked innocently.

"You need plenty of rest and will take the meds that the doctors prescribe."

There was no chance I'd risk rolling my eyes. The fear of the damn things falling out of my sockets seemed far too likely with the intensity of the pain.

He left without a word, returning I wasn't sure how long later since I'd closed my eyes once again. A middle-aged nurse was with him.

She offered me a broad smile, the corners of her eyes crinkling, lighting up her previously tired-looking face. "Morning, Dan. I'm Susie. How's your pain today on a scale of one to ten, one being you're ready to run a marathon, ten being you want to curl up in a ball and rock while throwing people off a cliff if they make too much noise?"

My snort was quickly followed by a fresh slice of pain. "Maybe a seven."

She bobbed her head as she checked my vitals, then passed me a few pills. "Here's an Endone and a couple of ibuprofen to get you started. The doctor has already started her rounds, so should be with you soon."

"Thanks." I swallowed back the pills, Ross at my side, helping me up and hovering. He then helped ease me back against my pillows.

Susie left us to it then. Ross settled on a different chair, one closer to my bed, his phone in his hand. "Just texting your mum, letting her know you're awake and we'll be seeing the doctor soon."

"Is everyone okay?" I asked, my throat nowhere near as scratchy as a few moments ago.

"Yeah, just worried."

"Craig, is he okay?" While I'd taken the brunt of the fall, I didn't know if he'd come off unscathed or not. He'd been at the hospital with me yesterday and had seemed okay, but I expected he'd been so focussed on me that he wouldn't look after himself properly.

"I think so. No injuries," Ross said quickly. I expected the haste was after seeing my expression morph with concern. "Just tired and overwhelmed, I think. You've all been under the hammer, going non-stop for weeks now. Yesterday shook him up." Ross paused, pulling his lips together and between his teeth.

I indicated for him to take my hand, under-standing quickly dawning on me. We'd all been shaken, not only the crew in attendance, but Ross and I expected my parents too. "I'm sorry you were worried." I kept my voice low, avoiding movement and too much noise. "But I'm okay." The doc had briefly spoken to Ross and me last night, reassuring us there was no bleeding or significant trauma to my brain.

Concussion was a fucker of a thing, though. I expected it would take a while to fully recover based on what the doctor had briefly explained yesterday before he'd left me to sleep.

The sound of Ross's swallow was hard, painful. He flicked his gaze away a beat before refocusing on me. "I know you're okay, and you have nothing to apologise for. None of this was your fault or anyone's fault." He squeezed my hand, an easy smile forming on his lips. "But I'd prefer it if you don't scare me shitless like that again."

I grinned, the movement slow and a little sappy as a gentle flow of warmth spread into my stomach, travelling across my limbs and caressing my sore brain.

"That Endone's kicking in, huh?"

"My head only feels like someone's splitting wood inside it rather than hacking at my brain."

Distress warred with amusement as Ross looked at me. "That doesn't sound exactly appealing."

I shrugged and could have whooped when the movement didn't cause of flash of fresh agony. "It's not great, but it's so much better than what it was."

His shoulders eased at my words, the action also helping me to relax more. I hated his distress, almost as much as I hated the situation I'd gotten myself in.

A thought struck me. "What day is it? Shouldn't you be at work?"

He shook his head. "Happy Australia Day."

I grunted, not at all surprised I'd lost track of the days, all seeming to bleed into one.

"School's going to be closed till next Monday. Staff not affected have been asked to meet tomorrow at nine, so they can go and help out any staff who've been impacted. Help with the clean-up and such."

"That's good."

"Yeah. It should help with morale and with everyone getting back on their feet."

I closed my eyes and exhaled, enjoying the ability to do so without the need to vomit. The door opening made me open my eyes, though it took a couple of attempts to do so, the drugs beginning to seriously work their magic.

"Morning, Dan. I'm Dr Lancaster. Are you still feeling a seven, or have those meds kicked in yet?"

"A pleasant three," I offered with a droopy smile, feeling like I'd knocked back more than a few beers and had reached that happy-drunk stage.

"That's good. They'll help you relax, help you

catch up with much-needed sleep so you can heal." She glanced at Ross, who remained seated and holding my hand. "Am I okay to discuss everything with your—" Her gaze dipped to our joined hands. "—boyfriend," she hedged, and it dawned on me she was looking for rings.

That thought had me pausing before my heart flipped over. And fuck if I'd forgotten about the monitor.

I jerked my attention at the monitor and then at Ross. Alarm crossed his features.

"What's wrong? Shit, are you okay?"

Heat slammed into my cheeks, and I was grateful as heck I felt high, else I would have perhaps handled it very differently. Instead, my drug-happy words had me answering, "It's okay, baby."

Ross's brows shot wide, and I grinned, realising I'd never called him *baby* or any other endearment. Huh, maybe that was something I'd have to change.

"You make my heart go flippety-flop," I continued, seriously happy with my ability to explain myself so clearly. "And then I started thinking about rings..." I trailed off, a new realisation hitting me. "I told you I loved you, but I didn't mean to. Not that I didn't mean to 'cause I really did, but not then. That was my sub... subc... my heart speaking to you.

'Cause I do, and maybe the ring idea would be good one day too. But we need more goat babies." I blinked slowly, once, twice, three times. "Bessie... are we already grandaddies? Is that weird, having grand-goats before kids. Ha." I chuckled, figuring I was so smart I made those punny things without even meaning to. "Kids, as in *kids* and baby goats."

My words dried up, but that was okay. My head was light, and I felt like I'd had a good night out on the town, drinking just enough to make me unbeliev-ably merry.

Movement to the right of Ross brought my atten-tion. I forced my focus away from his pretty face. "Oh, hey, Doc. Did you ask about Ross? He's my boyfriend."

Her lips twitched. "I kinda got that. It's probably best Ross stays, so he can remind you of *everything* discussed." She glanced at Ross and actually winked. I would have been pissed, but he deserved all the winks.

She then went on to talk about my head and my concussion. I simply latched on to me being discharged once I'd been to the bathroom and figured I could make that happen soon enough.

My gaze drifted to Ross as the doctor spoke. A light pink dusted his furry cheeks, and I wished I was closer so I could stroke them, but my arms felt heavy. My eyes closed, and I drifted off thinking about the soft scruff underneath my fingertips and how I wanted to think of the cutest pet name for Ross.

Relief wasn't even close to describing just how happy I was to be home.

The hospital staff had been great, incredible in fact, but Ross tucking me up in my own bed, then returning with a bowl of soup for us both was just the tip of perfection.

"Thanks." The scent of hearty beef and vegetable drifted over to me as I took the bowl off him.

"No worries," he said, still speaking quietly, aware my pain meds were wearing off. Making himself comfortable next to me, our backs pressed against the headboard and a bunch of fluffy pillows, he side-eyed me.

"You okay?"

"Yep, just be careful. It's piping hot."

I smiled. "I haven't forgotten how to eat food or test temperature," I said with amusement, not-so-secretly loving Ross's sweet attention.

"I'm more concerned about you spilling soup on your bed, or worse still, on yourself."

"Urgh, and probably right on my junk too. Hell no. I don't want a burnt dick."

He snorted. "I'd think you were starting to feel better, but I know otherwise." His gaze roamed my face, and I could just imagine what I looked like.

When he'd brought me home with the promise to look after me, since my folks were going to remain at his place and look after the animals, he'd helped me shower. Before I'd washed, I'd caught a glimpse of my haggard form, and honestly, post-shower, I didn't look too much better.

I kept quiet, blew gently on my soup, and started to shovel it in.

"You cool enough?"

"Yeah, thanks."

It was another scorching day, and I'd never been more grateful for the air conditioning unit in my bedroom. It made eating hot soup easier, that was for sure.

We ate in silence, a few sips, slurps, and only a couple of spills. Once done, Ross took away my bowl and returned with painkillers.

"How about taking some of these, and we'll both sleep?"

It was early afternoon, not that the time of day mattered in my condition. Nor in Ross's by the look of him. He appeared marginally better than me, but I expected his sleep had been all but non-existent in the hospital chair.

"Okay. Sleep I can do, especially if you're with me." The need in my statement was clear and earned me a soft smile. "And those Endone are pretty damn awesome."

When he chuckled, I raised my brow at him in question.

"You do get sorta drunk on them and loose-lipped."

"I do?" When I'd taken some, it hadn't taken long for my pain to ease and a sort of fog to settle in my brain. The whole effect had been a welcome relief.

Before I could think more about it, he passed me a glass of water. "Don't overwork that brain of yours. Just take these."

"How did I not know you were this bossy?" I asked with zero heat. He quirked his brow at me. "I like it," I sassed before swallowing the pills.

"Get used to it. I imagine you're going to take some reining in while you're healing."

"Me? Never."

"Uh-huh, and I'm Ryan Kwanten's secret lover."

I chuckled, ignoring the throb in my head. "Take that back."

"Perhaps if you promise to heal properly before doing... hell, anything, then I just might." He climbed into bed beside me and pulled the sheet up once I'd eased down next to him.

Rather than answering, I closed my eyes and breathed him in, relaxing even more when he wrapped his arm around me, holding me close.

"I missed you." He placed a kiss against my uninjured temple, and I sighed against his touch.

"Missed you too. It's been a wild few days."

"Weeks," he corrected.

"True."

The soft hum of the air conditioning unit filled the space. Beyond that, Ross's soothing breaths close to my face were the only other sound. Getting the chance to snuggle up to Ross again was the best, but I would have preferred it to be without the shitty situation or the brain-splitting concussion. But I wouldn't complain, not when his body heat was a familiar, welcoming comfort.

"You know I love you too, right?" he whispered.

I angled my neck to look at him. His eyes locked onto mine, a quiet intensity in their depths that spoke only of absolute conviction and love. The breath trying to escape my lungs caught in my throat, and it took a couple of times to remember how to loosen my muscles enough to breathe.

"You do?"

"Definitely." A small smile pulled at his lips. "So much."

My shoulders eased, my whole body relaxing at his words. "Good, 'cause I love the shit out of you."

He chuckled. "The shit, huh?"

"Well, perhaps a different image would be better."

"I'm good with sticking to a simple 'I love you.'"

I tried to turn, but he stopped me with a frown. I reluctantly gave in, secretly relieved, as the movement bloody hurt. Instead, he lifted up off the mattress so he was above me a little, still at my side.

"There's nothing simple about how I love you."

For the second time, he took my breath away, and all with a look before saying, "You can't say things like that to me when I can't do more than kiss you." An honest-to-God groan followed.

"You didn't believe me before."

"What's that?"

"That words can be my thing too."

The love in his eyes hit me square in the chest and he leaned closer.

Just as his lips were a hairsbreadth from mine, my eyes widened as a thought hit me. "Oh shit."

"What?" He edged away, his eyes roaming my face in concern.

"What did I say when the doctor asked about you?"

Ross's snicker told me enough and probably all I needed to know. The rest I expected I'd remember in time. But for now, I was happy to be silenced before my head became too fuzzy and I forgot what even a tongue could be used for.

"Just kiss me."

And he did.

23

—

ROSS

It took at least two weeks for a semblance of normality to filter through the town and our lives. There were still empty properties spread around town, places remaining unliveable, but on the whole, life carried on.

School had finally started after the hiccup of the delay. Dan was returning to work next week but would stick to the joinery shop rather than fitting for at least a week. Craig appeared back on form, having admitted he'd been struggling with the aftermath of disasters. He'd even mentioned talking to a professional to help him, which I was totally supportive of. And then there was the whole elephant in the room. Nick.

Perhaps one day we could be friends, but I was

nowhere near ready for that. We were polite, friendly even, and I happily let him bring his son by last weekend to see how the baby goats were getting on, and that was more than enough for the time being.

The positive was he respected that completely, and I no longer hesitated or caught my breath in the worst of ways when seeing him.

Even today, we'd invited him and his family around to Mum and Dad's for our delayed Australia Day celebrations. Dan had suggested the invite last week once we'd changed our get-together, and I hadn't even hesitated in agreeing that I thought it was a good idea.

"I swear to God, Dan, if you don't put that gas bottle down, I'm going to cause serious damage."

While I wasn't surprised Dan made a crappy patient, my threat was real. When having a "good" hour or so without a headache, he quickly forgot he had to take it easy.

"It's only a small one for the barbie."

I quirked my brow at him. "Are you seriously pouting and arguing about this?"

There was a beat of hesitation as he put the bottle down. "No. Not me." He followed up with a smirk, and I forgave him instantly.

I picked up the bottle, took it over to the barbeque and hooked it up. "Don't suppose you want to brave the kitchen and check if Mum needs help?" I asked over my shoulder, not realising he was standing close behind me. I smirked at how his stare lingered on my backside. "See something you like there?"

At my words, he adjusted himself, his shorts not doing a thing to disguise his hard-on. Yesterday was the first time we'd had sex since his accident. We'd been needy as hell to the point where it didn't take Dan much to convince me he was fine and his head wouldn't explode when he blew his load.

I'd all but pounced on him as soon as I agreed.

"My dick can't cope when you're on your knees like that. He gets ideas."

I snorted out a laugh, my own cock perking up at his interest and the thought of sucking Dan off. "Maybe we have enough ti—"

"Ross, can you come and grab the steaks" was hollered from the house.

I groaned. "Maybe not."

Dan twisted his lips, discomfort warring with amusement. "She asked for you, not me. There's no way I can go inside with this." He gave a hard squeeze of his dick, and I struggled to tear my attention away.

"Not helping," I mumbled, thinking of anything but the taste of Dan. I stood and adjusted myself. At least I had canvas shorts on, so I could shift my positioning a little. Dan's chuckle chased after me as I headed into the house. I flipped him off for good measure, still trying to will my hard-on to go down.

Helping Mum take things outside to the table did the trick of calming my libido. By the time I was filling up the Esky with more ice to keep the beer cold, Alec had arrived, and so had Nick, George, and their boy. Brie, Hannah, and their son, Nathan, had just pulled up and were getting out of their car.

I made my way over, Dan already there to greet them.

"You found the place okay?" I said, offering to take a covered plate off Hannah.

She handed it over. "Yeah, thanks. Sat nav got us right here. Ross, right?"

I grinned. "In the flesh. Pleased you could make it. And this must be Nathan." I smiled down at the little boy dressed in a brightly coloured tee and a unicorn horn hairband. "Wow, you didn't tell me you had a unicorn in your family."

The boy grinned widely at me. "My unicorn name is Princess Flower Poop."

Dan chuckled. "Cool name, Princess Flower Poop."

"It's pretty special," Brie said, closing the door and sending an amused smile our way.

"Let's head in out of the sun," I offered, keen to get Dan out of the bright light, all too aware he wasn't wearing his sunnies, which in the past had triggered a headache when outside.

We headed to my parents' wide veranda and placed the few plates on the three tables they'd put together to seat everyone. Dan was doing the introductions to his parents and mine, while Craig and Alec stood off to the side with George, beers in hand, talking and laughing at something. Alec was already bent low, saying something to Nathan and Murphy.

I stepped inside to grab the fan I'd forgotten to take outside earlier. Picking up the extension lead, I headed towards outside, only to be stopped by Dan, who was now in the kitchen.

"You okay?" I eyed him, concerned as he finished off a glass of water.

"Just took a couple of painkillers. Preventative if anything, so wipe that worry off your face."

He moved towards me, and we both glanced

outside when Alec's loud laughter caught our attention. Dan sidled up behind me, snaking his arms around my waist as I watched out the window at the group of people filling my parents' veranda.

"Quite a crowd out there," he mumbled close to my ear, then kissed on my neck.

"It's nice, right?"

I felt him bob his head, his chin settling on my shoulder. "You know, I remember that whole ring spiel."

It took a moment for his words to register, and I smirked. "You do, huh? It was one of your finer moments."

His strong arms squeezed my middle, and I sighed into his embrace.

"Perhaps one of my finer ideas too."

I froze at his words, which earned me a chuckle.

"Don't panic. I'm not saying right now."

While I heaved out a sigh, I wasn't entirely as relieved as perhaps my reaction indicated.

"I'm just saying this is nice, being with family, being with you. I love what we have but am excited about our future, you know?"

I placed the fan and lead down and turned in Dan's arms, my heart expanding. "I do know, and I'm sure we both want the same things, have the same plans."

He bobbed his head. "More baby goats and maybe a dog or two when I move in?"

My grin was instant and so wide it hurt. "You inviting yourself to move in?"

"Maybe. I still have a few months left on my lease, but having your kickarse kitchen as mine too wouldn't be so bad."

I chuckled and dotted a quick kiss to his mouth. "It is a pretty awesome kitchen. You should have seen the fitter."

"Was he hot?"

"The hottest."

"Did he have a big co—"

"Boys, are you heading back out? Your dad's burning the steaks. They need saving!" Mom called. Dad grumbled something in response, but Dan held most of my attention.

"The answer's yes." Elation swirled in my stomach, fluttering high and wrapping around my full heart.

"That I have a big cock?" Dan quirked his brow in question.

I rolled my eyes and flexed my fingers against his back, loving every inch of this man before me. "Well, yes, but on the other thing too, sharing my kitchen with you."

"Yeah?"

"Definitely."

His intense gaze pierced mine, need, desire, love burning brightly in their depths. "I love you," he whispered, his breath ragged.

"Love you," I said as he leaned in. I didn't keep him waiting, meeting him halfway in an instant.

Our lips connected with a soft groan escaping the both of us. Despite the need and urgency for more, our kiss remained gentle—soft lips, easy warmth, and a smooth stroke of tongues. We eased apart, my breathing shallow, and Dan's eyes blown.

The reverberation of more laughter outside drifted through the open door, and I smiled, happy to hear the sound despite the interruption.

"We best get out there before Mum sends Craig in to track us down."

"You lead and I'll follow."

He meant so much more than this single moment. I moved out of his embrace and held his hand, making a promise to let him know tonight that I would do exactly the same for him.

I'd do everything in my power to make sure this future we imagined would happen. And together, there was every chance we'd survive anything this life threw at us.

———

I hope you want to hug these guys as much as I do. I have such exciting news. ALEC has his very own story! Hooray. You can fall in love with Alec and his bi-awakening story in **Under the Blazing Stars**.

If you're looking for more low-angst M/M romance, check out my stand-alone book **Not Used To Cute**. Want something to get your heart pumping? Then **Thicker Than Water** should be next on your 1-click list. How about a new series to start? If so, my basketball are full of ridiculous antics in **No Take Backs**.

Thank you for reading!

ABOUT THE AUTHOR

Becca Seymour lives and breathes all things book related. Usually with at least three books being read and two WiPs being written at the same time, life is merrily hectic. She tends to do nothing by halves, so happily seeks the craziness and busyness life offers.

Living on her small property in Queensland with her human family as well as her animal family of cows, chooks, sheep, and dogs, Becca appreciates the beauty of the world around her and is a believer that love truly is love.

To check for updates head to Becca's website:
HTTPS://BECCASEYMOUR.COM
You can sign up for her newsletter here:
HTTPS://LANDING.MAILERLITE.COM/WEBFORMS/
LANDING/R9F0I4
Plus, join her Facebook group, which she shares with the awesome Louisa Masters here:
HTTPS://WWW.FACEBOOK.COM/GROUPS/
SEYMOURBOOKSWITHMASTERFULMEN/

facebook.com/beccaseymourauthor

twitter.com/beccaseymour_

instagram.com/authorbeccaseymour

bookbub.com/authors/becca-seymour

tiktok.com/@beccaseymourwrites

ACKNOWLEDGMENTS

A shout out to my superb editor, Liv Ventura, for always pushing me to be better and supporting me. My team at Hot Tree Editing are so awesome. Donna, you complete me!

Big cuddles to my incredible book designer who knows me so well and nails every design.

Finally, thanks to you, my wonderful readers, for taking a chance on one of my books.